Ginger
A Rainey Daye Cozy Mystery, book 8

by
Kathleen Suzette

Books by Kathleen Suzette:
A Rainey Daye Cozy Mystery Series
Clam Chowder and a Murder
A Rainey Daye Cozy Mystery, book 1
A Short Stack and a Murder
A Rainey Daye Cozy Mystery, book 2
Cherry Pie and a Murder
A Rainey Daye Cozy Mystery, book 3
Barbecue and a Murder
A Rainey Daye Cozy Mystery, book 4
Birthday Cake and a Murder
A Rainey Daye Cozy Mystery, book 5
Hot Cider and a Murder
A Rainey Daye Cozy Mystery, book 6
Roast Turkey and a Murder
A Rainey Daye Cozy Mystery, book 7
Gingerbread and a Murder
A Rainey Daye Cozy Mystery, book 8
Fish Fry and a Murder
A Rainey Daye Cozy Mystery, book 9
Cupcakes and a Murder
A Rainey Daye Cozy Mystery, book 10
Lemon Pie and a Murder
A Rainey Daye Cozy Mystery, book 11
Pasta and a Murder
A Rainey Daye Cozy Mystery, book 12
Chocolate Cake and a Murder
A Rainey Daye Cozy Mystery, book 13
A Pumpkin Hollow Mystery Series
Candy Coated Murder
A Pumpkin Hollow Mystery, book 1
Murderously Sweet
A Pumpkin Hollow Mystery, book 2
Chocolate Covered Murder

A Pumpkin Hollow Mystery, book 3
Death and Sweets
A Pumpkin Hollow Mystery, book 4
Sugared Demise
A Pumpkin Hollow Mystery, book 5
Confectionately Dead
A Pumpkin Hollow Mystery, book 6
Hard Candy and a Killer
A Pumpkin Hollow Mystery, book 7
Candy Kisses and a Killer
A Pumpkin Hollow Mystery, book 8
Terminal Taffy
A Pumpkin Hollow Mystery, book 9
Fudgy Fatality
A Pumpkin Hollow Mystery, book 10
Truffled Murder
A Pumpkin Hollow Mystery, book 11
Caramel Murder
A Pumpkin Hollow Mystery, book 12
Peppermint Fudge Killer
A Pumpkin Hollow Mystery, book 13
Chocolate Heart Killer
A Pumpkin Hollow Mystery, book 14
Strawberry Creams and Death
A Pumpkin Hollow Mystery, book 15
Pumpkin Spice Lies
A Pumpkin Hollow Mystery, book 16

A Freshly Baked Cozy Mystery Series
Apple Pie A La Murder,
A Freshly Baked Cozy Mystery, Book 1
Trick or Treat and Murder,
A Freshly Baked Cozy Mystery, Book 2
Thankfully Dead
A Freshly Baked Cozy Mystery, Book 3
Candy Cane Killer

A Freshly Baked Cozy Mystery, Book 4
Ice Cold Murder
A Freshly Baked Cozy Mystery, Book 5
Love is Murder
A Freshly Baked Cozy Mystery, Book 6
Strawberry Surprise Killer
A Freshly Baked Cozy Mystery, Book 7
Plum Dead
A Freshly Baked Cozy Mystery, book 8
Red, White, and Blue Murder
A Freshly Baked Cozy Mystery, book 9

A Gracie Williams Mystery Series

Pushing Up Daisies in Arizona,
A Gracie Williams Mystery, Book 1
Kicked the Bucket in Arizona,
A Gracie Williams Mystery, Book 2

A Home Economics Mystery Series

Appliqued to Death
A Home Economics Mystery, book 1

Table of Contents

Chapter One

"I'M SO EXCITED," NATALIE said looking at me from the passenger seat. "We are totally going to win this competition!"

I laughed. "Yes we are!"

My niece Natalie was home from college for winter break and was giddy with excitement at the prospect of winning the annual gingerbread house decorating contest. Sparrow, Idaho, is a small town, but we believe in community and events like this are one of the wonderful, charming events of the Christmas season.

It was something of an honor to win the contest although it was in name only. The prize awarded was a small trophy in the shape of a gingerbread house with the name of the event and the year won. There were only twelve teams of two people allowed to enter each year and it was on a first come, first serve basis. Of course, if you were one of those teams, you had to pay an entrance fee of two hundred and fifty dollars. The money went to buy toys for local underprivileged children for Christmas. It was expensive to compete in the contest, but it was well worth it to help local kids that might not otherwise have anything for Christmas.

"And we get to help the kids," she reminded me. "It's a win-win for everyone." She had a cute little floral ladybug canvas bag in her lap that held her cake decorating tools.

"I feel good about it too," I said as I pulled into the high school parking lot. "You've gotten really good at cake decorating. I think this is going to be a piece of cake." I chuckled at my own pun.

The gingerbread house contest would last most of the day. We had baked the pieces of the gingerbread house earlier in the morning, and when they had cooled down enough to handle, we used royal icing to put the house together. We were just getting back from the two-hour break in the middle of the day to begin the decorating. Natalie was in charge of most of the decorating. She had a lot of great ideas that I was sure would help us win the contest. Later, the three winning houses would be put on display at Santa's workshop near the fountain in the center of town.

We got out of the car and headed to the foods classroom. The local high school had small kitchenettes in the classroom with each kitchenette having a stove, microwave, and a small refrigerator. The cupboards were filled with supplies and we had been given a list of what would be provided so we knew what we needed to bring along with us.

Each team had to bake three extra cookies to be sampled by the judges because the house had to be as tasty as it was beautiful. I had a sure-fire recipe I had created to win over the judges. I was writing an Americana themed cookbook and the recipe would fit right in. Gingerbread houses may have originated in Germany, but Americans had made them a holiday tradition and added their own flair to them.

"I think I only got two hours of sleep last night, I was so excited," Natalie said as we strolled across the high school campus. She was dressed in a cute red and black tartan skirt, black tights, low-heeled black patent pumps, and a red sweater. She was cute as could be and in the Christmas spirit. It was the tenth day of December, and I was excited that she was home for the Christmas holiday. I had missed her.

"Are you going to be okay in those heels?" I asked, eyeing them. We would have an hour and a half to put the roof on the house and decorate it. That would be plenty of time to get the job done. The houses would be judged in the evening and then moved to Santa's workshop to display throughout the rest of the Christmas season. The workshop was a portable red and white metal shed that had been decorated for Christmas. There were gifts inside of it that could be purchased and the proceeds went to buy more toys for the children, and food for their families. Volunteers took in donations of toys and food, manning the workshop. Santa made an appearance every day.

"Yes, I think so. I'll slip them off if they bother me," she said, shifting the canvas bag of cake decorating tips and equipment from one shoulder to the other. I was thrilled that Natalie had recently gotten into cake decorating. She had plans to begin a small side business baking cakes, cupcakes, and cookies. She sold them for parties and as greeting cards to other college students. I was proud of her for creating her own business to help pay for college.

"I'm so excited about this," I said. I had worn athletic shoes so my feet wouldn't hurt while I worked. It had been too long since I wore heels regularly to be comfortable in them if I wore them for very long.

The foods classroom was warm and snug when we entered and we headed over to the corner kitchenette where we had left our gingerbread house to dry. We got some glances as we passed the other kitchenettes, but I didn't think anything of it until we got to ours.

Natalie gasped. "What happened?"

I stared in horror at the pieces of our gingerbread house on the floor in front of us. The walls of the gingerbread house had cracked, and it had come apart.

"Oh my gosh," I said kneeling down beside it. I looked over my shoulder at one of the judges, Susan Lang. "What happened to our house, Susan?"

Susan wrapped her arms around herself and came to the entrance of our kitchenette, peering at the pieces on the floor. Her short, curly brown hair had glitter spray in it and the tips had been dyed Christmas red.

She shook her head. "I don't know. I just saw it a few minutes ago. We left it because we thought it would be better if you handled the pieces."

"Well it didn't just fall off the counter by itself," I said. I heard the frustration in my voice, but I didn't care. Winning this contest meant a lot to Natalie, as well as myself, and I couldn't imagine how the gingerbread house had been knocked onto the floor.

"I really have no idea, Rainey," Susan said, sounding sympathetic. "I wish I could tell you what happened, but I can't. The pieces aren't terribly small. Perhaps you could put them back together with icing? You know, using it like glue?"

I felt anger rising up inside, and I bit my lower lip. "Who had access to this classroom? Was the classroom door locked while we took our break?"

She shrugged. "The door wasn't locked when I got back. I really don't know what happened. I'm sorry."

I turned back to look at the pieces on the floor and then at Natalie. She looked as if she were about to cry. I reached out a hand and placed it on her arm. "We'll figure something out. We can make more royal icing and glue the pieces together. It will work out."

"I'm sorry," Susan repeated and walked back to the two other judges.

"We can glue the pieces back together," I repeated to Natalie. "It will be fine." I said it as much for myself as for Natalie. I thought the royal icing would hold it together, but I couldn't swear that it would work with so little time for it to dry.

"I bet I know who did this," Natalie hissed as we picked up the pieces of the house and set them on the counter. She looked past me and over at Chrissy Jones.

Chrissy leaned against the counter in her own kitchenette and grinned. She looked like the cat that ate the mouse and I was pretty sure I knew who knocked our gingerbread house off the counter, too. Chrissy had been Natalie's best friend until they began junior high, but at the beginning of the seventh grade, she dumped Natalie without a second thought. It had been heartbreaking not only for Natalie but also for myself and her mother. The two had been close and Natalie had been completely dumbfounded by the turn of events.

"Uh-oh," a voice sang out behind us. "It looks like somebody's gingerbread house couldn't even withstand a couple of hours. I guess that's the way the cookie crumbles."

We looked to see Chrissy Jones standing at the entrance of our kitchenette. She had her arms folded across her chest and a smug smile on her face. I felt my blood boil.

"Did you need something, Chrissy?" I asked, turning to face her.

She shrugged. "Not really. I'm so sorry your gingerbread house got broken."

"And would you happen to know how that could have happened?" I asked.

She shook her head. "No, sorry. It was that way when we came back from our break." She turned and bounced back to her kitchenette. "Good luck!" she called over her shoulder.

"Let's try to ignore her," I said turning back to Natalie and looking over the damage. I didn't know if some of the pieces could handle the extra weight of the royal icing. Gingerbread house making was an art form, and I had only done it a few times.

I glanced in Chrissy's direction and saw her partner, Jenna Dennison, standing in their kitchenette, taking this all in. She looked unsure of what had just happened and I was willing to bet that Chrissy knew all about the broken gingerbread house, and Jenna was in the dark.

I could see Natalie's bottom lip tremble and I put a hand on her arm. "It will be fine, Natalie. It's just a little setback. Most of the pieces are pretty large, so I think it shouldn't be too difficult to fix. You just concentrate on what we're doing here, and we'll get it put back together again in just a few minutes."

Natalie nodded and turned away from Chrissy. We could hear some whispers and a giggle, but I shook it off. I was not going to let that snotty brat ruin this competition for us. Natalie had been looking forward to it ever since she went away to college in California last August. We had exchanged emails and pictures as Natalie practiced making gingerbread men and all kinds of cute scalloped designs with different sized frosting tips. I was not going to allow anyone to put a damper on her enthusiasm.

"We're going to win this," Natalie said, clenching her teeth together. She looked at me and I could see the renewed determination on her face. It made me proud. "We're going to win this thing, Aunt Rainey."

I nodded. "That's my girl," I said giving her a quick hug. "We are so going to win. And just think how sad Chrissy is going to be when we win with a broken gingerbread house."

Chapter Two

"I THINK IT TURNED OUT lovely," I said, trying to cheer Natalie up.

She wrapped her arms around herself, her eyes going to the floor for a moment and then she looked at me. I could see the unshed tears and it broke my heart. "It should have been so much better. And it could have been, if only it hadn't been broken."

I nodded. "I know. You're right, and I'm so sorry that happened. But I think we did a wonderful job putting the pieces back together and the decorating you did is beautiful." And it was. She had used frosting to create tiny flowers and frosted curlicues on the roof shingles. We had used plenty of candy on it, but the frosting touches really made the house look beautiful. We had tried to repair the large cracks in the walls, and we had covered the cracks nicely with frosting, but the royal icing we'd used as glue hadn't had enough time to dry. It was clear the roof was too heavy, and it started to sag in the middle by judging time. I was afraid it would collapse at any moment.

She sighed. "I guess there's always next year," she said.

"That's exactly right," I said brightly. "We'll try again next year." We had still managed to win fourth placed in the contest, but it was disappointing after looking forward to this for so long.

"It makes me angry that no one seems to know who broke our house, even though we know exactly who did it," she grumbled.

I agreed with her, but there wasn't anything we could do about it. And I certainly wasn't going to give up and quit, which was exactly what whoever was responsible for breaking our gingerbread house wanted us to do. Sure, we were fairly certain we knew who it was, but we had no proof.

"You're right, but this was all for charity, anyway. Our entrance fee is going to a good cause, and other than the house getting broken, we had fun planning it out, didn't we?"

She smiled and nodded. "We did. I think we make a good team, and next year we're going to win."

"We certainly will," I said. "Let's go get a coffee."

THE THREE WINNING GINGERBREAD houses were brought to the fountain at Center Plaza. A table had been set up to display them inside Santa's workshop for the rest of the Christmas season. The fountain itself had been turned off and drained and a winter wonderland complete with lighted penguins and polar bears had been set up inside of it.

There would be something going on at Center Plaza every evening through Christmas Eve. The high school chorus would sing a couple of nights, as well as various church choirs. I had also seen an announcement that there would be short plays put on by the grammar schools on a couple of different nights. The city had decorated the streets around the fountain and the plaza and it felt like a mini winter wonderland. All the nearby shops had put up their best Christmas finery in the spirit of the season and there were also bake sales held by local churches to benefit worthy causes. I was so glad I had moved home from New York City earlier in the year. I missed the small town holiday excitement.

My identical twin sister, Stormy, my mother, Natalie, and I were busy looking through the gift shop near Center Plaza the next evening. I had already seen where the gingerbread houses were on display and it made me a little sad that ours wasn't there. Chrissy and Jenna's gingerbread house had won first place. It left a sour taste in my mouth and I knew it bothered Natalie, but there wasn't anything we could do about it.

"I absolutely love this snow globe," Stormy said picking it up to show me. She wound the bottom of it and it began playing *Silent Night*. Inside the globe, snow dropped on a stable scene. The entire globe lit up, and it had a bright starry sky in the background. It was quite striking.

"That's really pretty," I said, looking at it. "I love the silver work on the base." The base was heavy with silver colored metal that had been molded with pretty curly cues and swirls.

"Oh, Natalie," Stormy said turning to her. "This sure is a pretty snow globe, isn't it?"

Natalie turned to look, and grinned. "It is. Whoever gets that for Christmas sure is going to be happy."

"Yes, whoever gets it would be *delighted* to receive it," Stormy said putting emphasis on delighted.

"Sadly, I've done most of my Christmas shopping already," Natalie said shrugging.

"Oh," Stormy said sadly and set the snow globe back on the shelf.

"I haven't finished my shopping yet," I said. "I wonder if I know someone that would like a snow globe?"

Stormy gave me a cheesy grin. "I bet you do know someone that would love a snow globe."

"I guess that person better be really good or Santa won't bring it to her," I said and walked away from the snow globe.

"Oh, she is! She is very good," Stormy said following after me. "I still don't know what to get Bob. I hate getting him the same thing every year."

"What do you get him that's the same?" I asked.

"Tools, or clothes. I don't know, I guess I don't actually get him the same thing every year, but it feels that way. I want to give him something special this year. I wish I had a clue what that might be."

"We're running out of time, so if you're going to get him something special, you better get working on it." I had no room to talk. I still hadn't bought my boyfriend Cade anything. But I had an excuse. We'd only been dating a few months, and I wasn't sure what he would like.

"I'd like a new car," Mom said, coming up behind us. In her hand was a box of red glass ball ornaments.

"Well you better tell Santa then," Stormy said. "Because his little elves don't have money for a new car."

"His little elves need to get better jobs," Mom said.

I chuckled. "I would totally get you a brand-new car if I could afford it," I said. "I appreciate you helping me to get into my house and it would be the least I could do for you."

"The least you could do for me is right," Mom said, picking up a crystal icicle that had a red satin ribbon to hang it with.

"Are we about ready to move on to the next shop?" Stormy asked.

"I am," I said. The gift shop had a lot of beautiful things to look at, but I hadn't selected anything yet. I had always had trouble making decisions about gifts.

"I'll pay for my ornaments, and then we can go," Mom said.

When Mom finished paying for her ornaments, we headed for the door. I decided I would slip back later and pick up that snow globe for Stormy. I was pretty sure she knew I would get it for her, but I didn't want to buy it in front of her. Let her wonder.

As we stepped out into the cold, I pulled my coat close around me. That was when a scream pierced the night. Everyone stopped and looked in the direction of the fountain.

"What's going on over there?" Natalie asked.

"I don't know, but I'm going to find out," I said, hurrying over to Santa's workshop. There was a young woman backing away from the table that the gingerbread houses sat on, a look of horror on her face. She screamed again. I tried to move quickly without slipping on the icy sidewalk. "What's going on?" I called as I got closer.

The table was covered in a long red tablecloth that touched the ground. The girl looked at me and shook her head, pointing at a spot near the bottom of the tablecloth. I hurried over to the other side of the table, but the tablecloth touched the ground and I didn't see anything. I looked at the girl. A volunteer was behind the counter in Santa's workshop, and Santa sat on his chair. The two watched what was going on, but neither moved.

"Under there," the girl breathed out.

I hesitated, then kneeled down and lifted the skirt of the tablecloth. Chrissy Jones lay beneath the table, her glassy eyes staring up at the bottom of the table. I inhaled sharply, the cold air hurting the back of my throat. I stared at her for a moment, then reached a hand out to her wrist and felt for a pulse. She was ice cold and blood pooled onto the floor from beneath her head. I quickly released the tablecloth and stood up as people gathered around.

"What's going on?" a man said from behind me.

Without answering him, I pulled my phone from my pocket and quickly dialed Cade.

When he answered I let my breath out. "Cade, you need to come down to the Center Plaza. There's been an accident." Chrissy had had more than an accident, but I didn't want to go into detail with people standing around and listening to my conversation.

"What kind of accident?" he asked.

"A serious accident, the kind that you handle," I said, speaking in code.

"Seriously?" he asked.

"I wish I wasn't," I said. "You need to hurry down here. There are a lot of people milling about."

"There's a dead body?" he asked for clarification.

"Yes," I said, glancing at the people gathering around me now.

"I'll be right there. Try to keep people from walking through the crime scene or seeing the body," he said and ended the call.

I turned around and looked at the crowd that was gathering. "I need you all to back up, please. It looks like there's been an accident and the police will be here any moment."

"What's going on, Rainey?" Stormy asked in a whisper as she came to stand beside me. Her long blond hair had come out from beneath her knit hat and she pushed it away from her face.

I shook my head. "Cade will be here any minute." I looked past Stormy to Natalie. Her eyes were wide, and she was biting her bottom lip.

Chapter Three

"RAINEY," I HEARD FROM behind me. "What's going on?"

I turned around to see my boss, Sam Stevens, coming toward me, his face questioning. Sam owned Sam's Diner, and I was a waitress there.

"Sam," I said with relief. "There's been an accident. Cade is on his way."

He moved close to me. "I heard someone scream," he whispered. "What happened?"

"There's a body beneath the table," I whispered back, my eyes cutting to the table that held the gingerbread houses. "We need to keep it quiet. Can you help me clear the area?"

He nodded. "Okay folks," he said, turning to the gathering crowd. "We need to clear the area. The police will be here any minute."

"I saw a dead body," the girl who had screamed said. She looked to be about sixteen and I was sorry she had seen Chrissy in the state she was in, but she needed to be quiet. The last thing Chrissy's parents needed was for talk of their dead daughter being spread around town before they even knew she was gone.

I groaned. "We're going to wait for the police and they'll take care of everything," I assured her. "Why don't you have a seat on the bench near the fountain until they come. I'm sure they'll want to speak with you."

She looked at me wide-eyed. "Why? Why would they want to speak to me? I was just walking past the table looking at the gingerbread houses and I dropped my phone. It landed partway under the tablecloth and when I brushed the tablecloth, I saw a finger. I swear that's all that happened." She shook her head, her eyes still wide with shock.

There was a murmur from behind me and I wished she would be quiet about the body. I needed her to wait for Cade without panicking herself and the crowd, but I wasn't sure how I was going to achieve that. "I understand completely. Why don't you have a seat," I repeated.

"Who was it?" a woman asked the girl. "Who did you see down there? What happened?"

I sighed. "Look, we don't know anything right now. I need everyone to step back." Most people stood right where they were when I said it. Crowd control didn't seem to be my strong suit.

"Who is it?" the woman repeated.

The girl looked at the woman and shrugged. "I don't know. I didn't take a good look at her. I just saw someone was under the table and I think I saw some blood."

The woman looked at me. "I want to know who's under there. What if it's someone I know?"

"If it's someone you know, do you really want to see them like that? The police are going to handle this," I repeated firmly.

She thought about what I'd just said and took a couple of steps back, nodding. "Okay then. I'll wait for the police."

Stormy, my mother, and Natalie were hanging back near the fountain and I looked at them and shook my head. Natalie wrapped her arms around herself and looked at me, questioningly. I wondered how Natalie would react when she found out it was Chrissy beneath the table and that she had been murdered.

Most of the crowd still hadn't left. Cade was going to have a job keeping these people in line. I heard sirens in the distance and I heaved a sigh of relief. I needed Cade to take charge.

The woman that was volunteering at the workshop walked over to me. The shocked look on her face said she had no idea Chrissy was beneath the table. "I don't know how she got there," she whispered. "Honest. I got here an hour and a half ago. I didn't see a thing."

"How long has this table been set up?" I asked.

"We put it up last night when they brought the gingerbread houses over. I don't know how this could have happened." She shook her head sadly. "Is she dead?"

I smiled without answering. My mind turned with thoughts. Where was Chrissy last night? Had she stopped by to see her gingerbread house on display? Who had keys to Santa's workshop?

Sam kept trying to direct people away from the workshop and Chrissy's body, but most people just stepped back a few feet and refused to leave the area. Some grumbled about being asked to leave, but moved away without being forced.

Cade parked his car in the parking lot closest to the fountain and jumped out, striding quickly toward me.

"What's going on?" he asked when he got to me.

"She's under there," I said, pointing to the tablecloth.

Cade went to the far side and knelt beside the table, lifting the tablecloth just enough to see beneath it. He reached for Chrissy's wrist and took her pulse. "She's been gone for a while."

"That's what I thought," I whispered. I was relieved when uniformed officers pulled up and headed in our direction. "The troops are here."

"Clear the area," Cade ordered the first uniformed officer that got to us.

The officers began surrounding the plaza and directing people back, away from the area. They quickly put up crime scene tape so people wouldn't wander closer. It was amazing how quickly the crowd moved when it was the police directing them to do it.

I went to Stormy. "Why don't you take Mom and Natalie home and I'll call you later," I said.

She nodded. "Let me know if you need me to come and pick you up," she said without asking who was beneath the table.

I headed back over to Cade. "What did you see?" Cade asked, lowering his voice.

"The young girl sitting there by the fountain screamed, and I came to see what was going on. This is what I found. The woman working at Santa's workshop said she didn't see a thing."

There was a uniformed officer already speaking to the young girl. He had his notebook out and was taking down her statement.

"Do you know the girl beneath the table?" he asked.

I nodded. "It's Chrissy Jones. She was in the gingerbread house decorating contest yesterday. She won first place."

He looked at me, one eyebrow raised. "Wait a minute. Chrissy Jones? Wasn't she a suspect in another murder?"

"Yes she was. Pamela North's murder," I said.

He considered this, then turned back to her. "It looks like someone hit her on the head with something heavy," Cade said, examining the wound. "We'll have to wait for the coroner to come. But for now, this area has to be closed down."

It was a shame, but I understood. The Christmas season for Sparrow was a busy one and it would mean the nearby businesses would be affected. "Do you think the Plaza will be opened by tomorrow night?"

He shrugged. "I would imagine, but I can't swear it will." He pulled his coat closer against a cold breeze. "I just hope the coroner gets here quickly. It's getting awfully cold."

I nodded. "Kind of a bummer for the Christmas season, isn't it?"

He nodded. "It is. But it's even more of a bummer for Chrissy Jones."

That was the truth. When Chrissy and Natalie were young, I had known Chrissy's family well. But when the girls broke off their friendship, I hadn't seen Chrissy's parents much. It broke my heart that the chubby-cheeked little girl I used to know was laying dead beneath a table.

I watched as Cade made the call to the coroner and then made another call to the police station. The night sky was clear and stars twinkled overhead, but it was bitingly cold with a breeze that intensified the freezing temperature.

"You probably need to go on home," Cade said when he got off the phone. "We'll probably have a long wait before the coroner gets here. There's no use you standing out here freezing with me."

"I don't want to leave you alone," I said stubbornly. I pulled up the collar of my coat to shield myself from the wind. "How about I go down to the coffee shop and pick up some coffee for you and the other officers?"

He nodded. "I'm sure that would be much appreciated."

There was a coffee shop within walking distance. It wasn't my friend Agatha Broome's coffee shop, but Stormy had driven us to go shopping and I was now without a car. Her shop was too far away. I hurried over to the coffee shop on the corner and went in. There had been four uniformed officers that showed up so far and I decided to go ahead and order eight coffees in case more showed up by the time I got back.

"What's going on out there?" The girl behind the counter asked me.

I shrugged. "I'm not really sure," I lied. I didn't want to spread around the news about a dead body in Santa's workshop. "I guess there might have been an accident of some sort." I put in my order for the eight coffees and ordered creamer and sugar on the side.

"Hey Rainey," Sam said, coming into the coffee shop. "Kind of crazy out there, huh?"

I turned and nodded. "You can say that again. I'm picking up some coffee for the officers. I appreciate your help out there."

He nodded. "They're going to need the coffee to warm up. I'm sure they'll be out there for a while," he said.

"Here you are," the barista said, setting the cups of coffee on the counter. She had put them into cardboard carriers and loaded them up with packets of creamer and sugar for me.

"Thanks." I picked up the cardboard carriers with the coffee and headed toward the door.

Sam held the door open for me. "Is that who I think it is under that table?" he whispered.

"Maybe," I said and mouthed Chrissy's name. "Let's keep it quiet though. I'd hate for her family to find out from someone other than the police."

He nodded. "What a shame. So close to Christmas, too."

I nodded. "You can say that again. Thanks for opening the door for me." I headed through the door and back to Cade.

When I got to him, he took one of the coffees and signaled to the uniformed officers to come and get one. I shivered and took one of the coffees for myself. Cade might make me go home at some point in time, but for now, I was going to hang out and see what was going on. You can call me nosy, but I felt like I had a vested interest here. Chrissy had been Natalie's best friend for years after all.

"Any ideas on what might have happened here?" he asked me.

I shook my head. "Not a clue. But a funny thing happened at the gingerbread house contest today. When Natalie and I returned after the break for the decorating portion of the contest, somebody had knocked our house on the floor and broke it."

He lifted one eyebrow. "Someone broke your house?"

I nodded. "Chrissy and Natalie were friends when they were younger, but they had a falling out in the seventh grade. Chrissy sure was happy about our house getting broken, and if I had to bet on something, I would bet that she was the one who did it."

"That's odd," he said. "But, I guess that's the way the cookie crumbles." He grinned.

I narrowed my eyes at him. "You're such a comedian. And it's funny because Chrissy said the exact same thing yesterday."

"Great minds think alike I guess," he said.

I rolled my eyes at him. "Smarty. Don't you have some investigating to do?"

"That I do."

I sighed. I didn't know who would want to kill Chrissy Jones, but I was going to find out.

Chapter Four

BY EIGHT O'CLOCK MY toes were nearly frozen solid, to say nothing of the tip of my nose feeling like if I touched it, it would snap right off my face. Cade insisted one of the uniformed police officers take me home, and as much as I hated to leave him out in the cold while I went home and enjoyed a nice warm fire, I finally agreed. I didn't think I'd like going through life missing my nose or any of my toes.

I knew Stormy was waiting to hear from me. I had to give her credit for being patient and not texting me to find out what was going on. I had the uniformed officer drop me off at her house so I could fill her in on what little I knew.

Stormy opened the door and looked at me wide-eyed. "I was wondering where you were!" she said, stepping back so I could come inside.

The warmth of the house made me groan with delight. I made a beeline over to the fireplace and slipped the gloves off my hands so nothing blocked the heat from getting to them. "This feels so good. You have no idea," I said.

"So what happened? Tell me what's going on," Stormy said, following me over to the fireplace.

"It was Chrissy."

"Hi Bob," I said to my brother-in-law.

"Hey, Rainey. Sorry to hear someone died tonight," he said, laying down the newspaper he had been reading.

"It's a terrible shame," I said.

"Aunt Rainey," Natalie said coming in from the kitchen. "It was Chrissy? What happened to her?"

I groaned again from the delicious warmth of the fireplace. "I really don't have any idea yet. All I know is Chrissy had a head wound and someone put her under the table."

"What's going on in here?" Mom said, coming in from the kitchen with a cup of cocoa in her hand. "What happened to Chrissy Jones?"

"Mom, what are you doing here?" I asked.

"Did you think I was just going to go home and go to bed? I knew you'd tell Stormy what's going on, and I want to know too. Now spill it."

"Like I just said, Chrissy Jones is dead. She had a head wound and I don't know anything else."

"How sad," Natalie said staring into the fire. "I wonder what happened to her?"

"It's too early to know anything, but Cade will figure it out," I said. "It's weird. She just won the gingerbread decorating contest yesterday and now she's dead."

"What's weird about that?" Mom asked. "Is there a rule that you can't be murdered the day after you win a gingerbread house decorating contest?"

I shrugged. "I don't know. I guess it's just because we saw her and talked to her yesterday, and now she's gone. It just feels like a shock is all."

"You don't expect people you know to be murdered," Bob said.

"Maybe she fell and hit her head on the ice? Or concrete?" Mom suggested. "Did you think of that? The sidewalks have been icy and slippery."

"And then she just happened to roll beneath the table that the winning gingerbread houses were on?" I asked, trying to keep the sarcasm out of my voice and failing.

"I'm pretty sure that didn't happen, Mom," Stormy said, sounding uncharacteristically sarcastic. Sarcasm was my forte, not Stormy's. "Did Cade say anything about what he thinks happened?"

I shook my head. "I'm sure it'll be a day or two before he knows anything for certain. He was still waiting on the coroner to come and pick up her body. It's freezing out there. I hated to leave him in the cold like that."

"It seems weird that somebody I was best friends with for so many years is dead," Natalie said still staring into the fireplace. Her lips formed a hard line, and she sighed heavily.

"You can say that again," Stormy said. "We used to do so many fun things with her and her parents. I feel terrible for Carol and Roger. I just can't imagine losing a child."

"You know what's weird?" Natalie asked, looking at me now.

"What?" I asked.

"It was really weird that she and Jenna Dennison were partners for the gingerbread contest. They hated each other in school. I mean, really hated each other. When I saw them together, I just couldn't understand it."

"Define hated each other," I said.

"When Chrissy and I split up, the two of them became best friends, but that only lasted about a year. When Jenna stole Chrissy's boyfriend in the eighth grade, it was all out war after that. They were always fighting. They hated each other. Chrissy kept spreading rumors about Jenna, but Jenna really wasn't any better. She sabotaged Chrissy's science project one year by writing something ugly on the poster board she was using for her presentation."

That made me think about our broken gingerbread house. "Did you ever have problems with Jenna?"

Natalie shook her head. "We hung around together for a while, but it wasn't long. She was nice. I always figured it was Chrissy causing all the trouble between them." She shrugged. "And maybe it was."

I nodded, taking this in. "Do you know for sure that she was the one that sabotaged Chrissy's science project?"

She nodded. "She tried to get me to help her, but I told her I didn't want any trouble."

"Oh the drama of teenage girls," Mom said. "It seems like you all are always having issues." Mom was one to talk. She owned a flower shop and she'd had her own drama with other business owners from time to time.

"Not me," Natalie said. "I always tried to stay away from girls that caused a lot of drama. That made it easy not to be friends with Chrissy because she was one of the biggest drama queens in the school."

"Did Chrissy ever want to be friends with you again?" I asked.

She nodded and smiled. "She did. I guess it was a slap in the face when I told her I wasn't interested. Like I said, I tried to stay away from drama queens."

"I know you've always tried to avoid that kind of trouble," Stormy said putting an arm around Natalie's shoulders. "I'm sure Cade will get it sorted out and arrest her killer."

Chrissy had had issues with a former murder victim, Pamela North, several months earlier. When I had asked around about Pamela's death, Chrissy had been at the top of my list of possible suspects for a while. At the time it seemed that Pamela might have caused all the trouble between the two of them, but now I wondered. Both Pamela and Chrissy had been beauty pageant contestants, and they both lived up to their reputations as drama queens.

"I know it was hard on you at first when she broke off your friendship," I said to Natalie.

She looked at me and shook her head. "I don't have any regrets. After what Chrissy did to me, I haven't had any feelings about her for years."

"What exactly did she do?" Mom asked and took a sip of her cocoa.

Natalie looked away. "I'd rather not say."

"That's okay, Natalie," I said. "You don't need to say what it was. Sometimes things just don't work out. And I'm sure with all the prepubescent hormones going on at the time, and with Chrissy and her beauty queen stuff, you were better off without her."

She nodded and went back to staring at the fire. She may have said it didn't bother her that Chrissy was dead, but I had a hunch that wasn't the full truth.

"I probably should drop in on Chrissy's parents in the next couple of days and pay my respects," Stormy said. "It wouldn't be right if I didn't. We were close at one time. Bob, can you go with me?"

"I wish I could, but I've got meetings all this week," he said.

"I can go with you if you want me to," I offered.

"That would be nice. I feel bad that I haven't had much contact with Carol since the girls stopped being friends. I guess I dropped my friendship with her and Roger when the girls dropped theirs, if that makes any sense."

"I can understand that," I said. "If I remember right, things were kind of crazy back then. All of that junior high school excitement."

Carol Jones had been a nice person. I hadn't known her quite as well as Stormy had, but I could see why the friendship had ended if the girls couldn't get along anymore.

I pulled my phone from my pocket and fumbled with it. My fingers were still a little stiff from the cold. It was wishful thinking hoping Cade would text me. He would be busy for the rest of the night. I slipped my phone back into my pocket. "Do you have any snacks, Stormy?" All of a sudden I felt like I could eat a horse.

"I've got some chocolate chip cookies and some cocoa," she said and led the way to the kitchen.

"Aunt Rainey!" My niece Bonney said, running to me. I turned around and caught her up in a hug.

"How are you doing, Bonney?" She was dressed in red onesie pajamas and looked like she had slipped out of bed.

"Good," she said taking hold of my hand. "Your hands are cold, and I want a chocolate chip cookie."

"I knew you had ulterior motives for getting out of bed," I said and laughed.

It was a shame that Chrissy Jones had died, and even worse that it was so close to Christmas. I knew Cade would do everything he could to find her killer as quickly as he could, but it would ruin the holiday for her family for the remainder of their lives.

Chapter Five

I STOPPED BY STORMY'S house the following afternoon. We had planned on driving over to see Chrissy's parents, Carol and Roger Jones, and offer our condolences. I had baked a white chocolate Christmas torte to take to them.

Natalie opened the door and gave me a smile. "Hi Aunt Rainey," she said.

"Hi Natalie," I said, stepping into the warm house. We hadn't gotten any more snow, but the temperatures had dropped overnight and I was feeling the chill. I followed Natalie into the living room where the fireplace was crackling. "Are you and your mom ready to go see Chrissy's parents?"

She turned to look at me. "No, I'm not going with you and Mom."

That surprised me. "You're not?"

She shook her head. "I just can't. I don't think it would be appropriate."

I looked at Natalie for a moment. She fidgeted and looked away.

"Are you sure? I know it's been years since you and Chrissy were friends, but Carol and Roger were always sweet people."

Her eyes met mine. She shook her head and looked away. "I would rather not."

"Hi Rainey," Stormy said, walking into the living room. "I guess I'm ready to go see Carol and Roger."

"Natalie said she isn't going with us," I said to her.

Stormy shrugged. "That's what she told me earlier. Why don't we get going?"

"You're sure, Natalie?" I asked before we headed out.

"I'm sure. I think it's better that I don't." She sat on the couch and turned the television on.

I hesitated, then followed Stormy out of the house. There was no use arguing with her if she really didn't want to go. When the front door was closed behind us, I turned to look at Stormy. "How has she been doing?"

Stormy shrugged. "She doesn't really want to talk about it. To be honest, I just think it's been a terrible shock to her. Even though they hadn't been chummy in forever, I've always felt she still had feelings for her old friend. I think there were times that she just missed her. They were so tight at one time."

"I guess that makes sense," I said, getting into my car. "When you're young, it's always a shock to know somebody that suddenly dies. And since this is a murder, I think that makes it more shocking."

CAROL AND ROGER LIVED in a newer home on the south side of town. I sighed as I parked my car and looked at the house. There was a snowman on the front lawn and Christmas lights along the edge of the roof. Two large Christmas wreaths brightened the double front doors and colored lights lined the front windows. A couple of pine trees in the front yard had lights strung on them and a small nativity scene sat on the corner of the front porch. It was simple and understated. "Well, I guess we may as well go in," I said after a few moments and got out of the car.

I reached into the back seat and got the Christmas torte and we headed up the driveway. Stormy rang the doorbell and we waited.

"Oh," Carol Jones said when she answered the door. "Stormy, Rainey. I wasn't expecting you." Her eyes went to the bakery box in my hands and she forced herself to smile.

I suddenly felt awkward. I hadn't expected her to be overjoyed at seeing us, but I wasn't expecting her to be so detached toward us.

"Carol," Stormy said, "we're so sorry to hear about Chrissy. We just wanted to stop by and offer our condolences."

She nodded. "Of course," she said and stepped back. "Won't you come in for a moment?" We followed her into the living room and she motioned for us to have a seat. "I can't visit long. We've got arrangements to make."

I nodded and tried not to glance at Stormy. "We won't keep you long. I made a white chocolate Christmas torte," I said holding the box out to her.

"That was so sweet of you," she said, taking the box from me. "Let me put this in the kitchen."

I glanced at Stormy and she gave me a slight shrug. We hadn't meant to make Carol uncomfortable. In her absence, we looked around the room. There were pictures of Chrissy on the walls, the piano, and the coffee table. The pictures went from when she was a baby to more recent photos as she posed in her pageant dresses. Chrissy had been an only child, and I knew that would make the loss felt more keenly. Not that it would have mattered if there were ten other children, but it might make life a little bleaker without another child to fill the hole Chrissy had undeniably left.

"It was kind of you both to think of us," Carol said coming back into the room and sitting on the sofa across from us. "I don't know what Roger and I are going to do." She seemed to have relaxed and when she looked up at us, there were tears in her eyes.

"Carol, I just can't tell you how sorry I am. I can't imagine what the two of you are going through," Stormy said.

"It's terrible," I echoed. "I'm so sorry."

She nodded. "Thank you," she said, sounding more like the old Carol we used to know. "I'm afraid we're still in shock. Roger hasn't come out of our bedroom since we heard. I don't know what we're going to do without our Chrissy."

"I wish there was something we could say or do that would make things at least a little easier, but I know there isn't anything that will help," I said.

She nodded. "What I don't understand is how someone could do something so terrible. Chrissy was the sweetest girl. But I guess I don't need to tell the two of you that, do I? You remember her and what a wonderful little girl she was, don't you?" She looked at us imploringly.

We both nodded. "She really was a sweet girl," Stormy said.

And she really had been when she was very young. There was no sense in bringing up how nasty she had been when she decided she didn't want to be Natalie's friend anymore. Right now, Chrissy's mother was suffering from the loss of her only child and I wasn't going to cause her more pain.

"I was so proud of her when she called me and said she won the gingerbread decorating contest. She was practically giddy when she came home and showed me the trophy. I didn't think Chrissy had any baking ability, but I guess I was wrong. Her partner Jenna did the decorating, but Chrissy did the baking. Did you see it?"

"I did," I said glancing at stormy. "Actually, Natalie and I were also in the contest. And you're right, Jenna did a beautiful job decorating that gingerbread house."

She nodded and bit her lip. "So Natalie was in the contest?"

I nodded. "Yes, she was. She did the decorating for our team."

She thought about this for a moment, then she looked at me. "Chrissy told me that Natalie hated her. She said when they were in the ninth grade Natalie tried to humiliate her in front of the whole class."

I was shocked. Natalie wasn't the sort of girl that would try to humiliate anybody.

"What do you mean she tried to humiliate her in front of their class?" Stormy asked. She sounded as shocked as I was.

"I suppose I shouldn't bring it up," Carol said, looking down at her hands. "But they had a science class together, and they were all doing projects. Chrissy and her partner had used a tri-fold poster board to show the steps to making a battery.

They actually made one and hooked it up to a little car to make it work. On the day they were supposed to demonstrate their project, they opened up the poster board and Natalie had written in red felt marker that Chrissy was sleeping with one of the boys in the class." She looked up at us. "My Chrissy wasn't that kind of girl."

I stared at her wide-eyed. I was certain she had to be wrong. "Are you sure?" I asked her. "That doesn't sound like Natalie."

She nodded. "I wanted to go to the principal and complain about what happened, but Chrissy wouldn't let me. She said the teacher had already dealt with the problem and she didn't want to make it a bigger deal than it already was. She was humiliated. I understand the two had a falling out, but you would have thought that by two years later, Natalie would have gotten over it."

"I'm so sorry," Stormy said. "This is the first I've heard of this. I've never known Natalie to behave that way."

"I'm sure it's a shock," Carol said. "And I shouldn't even be bringing it up, but when Rainey said Natalie was in the gingerbread competition, it just brought back that memory." She laughed sadly. "How stupid for something like that to come to me now, right?"

I sat back on the sofa and took this in. Was that why Natalie didn't want to come with us to speak to Carol and Roger? I couldn't reconcile what Carol had just told us with what I knew of Natalie.

"Did Natalie confess to the teacher that she did it?" I asked her. Natalie had said it was Jenna that sabotaged Chrissy's project.

"Yes, the teacher said she confessed to it," Carol said, nodding. "But let's forget about that. I'm so sorry I brought it up. It really doesn't make any difference now, does it?"

I shook my head slowly. "No, I guess it doesn't."

"If you want to know the truth, the only person I can think of that might have wanted to harm my Chrissy," she said, "was her partner in the gingerbread decorating contest. Jenna Dennison. But even so, I still can't imagine her actually doing something like killing her."

"Why do you say that?" I asked.

"The only person that hated Chrissy more than Natalie," she said, "was Jenna. They were rivals all through junior high and high school and I can't tell you the number of times Chrissy came home crying about something Jenna had done."

"Then why did they become partners?" I asked her. Natalie had said the same thing about Chrissy and Jenna. They hated each other. But why would Carol think Natalie had written something ugly on her science project?

She shrugged. "I asked Chrissy that several times. But all she would say is that she and Jenna had put their differences behind them and Jenna was excellent at decorating cakes and cookies. She said she intended to win the contest. I still can't get over the fact that she's gone. She never even got to enter the Miss America pageant. We were so looking forward to that. She would have won. I know she would have." She sniffed and reached for a tissue from the box on the coffee table.

I looked at Carol. It seemed odd that Chrissy had wanted to win the gingerbread decorating contest badly enough that she partnered with someone she didn't like. I had to wonder what her motivation was.

We stayed and talked to Carol a while longer and then excused ourselves.

"The only person that hated Chrissy more than Natalie?" Stormy said once we got back into my car. "Natalie doesn't hate Chrissy! She was over their breakup years ago." Stormy harrumphed as she fastened her seatbelt. "Natalie was at home all evening after the gingerbread house contest, and she stayed there until we went shopping the following evening. Even if she had wanted to kill chrissy, she was at home. She couldn't have done it."

"I know, right? I didn't expect this visit to go the direction it did. You and I both know there's no way Natalie could have done anything to hurt Chrissy."

She nodded and stared out the window. "I know my girl. She would never have written something like that on Chrissy's project poster board and embarrassed her like that, either. And why would Carol bring that up now?"

I started my car and pulled away from the curb. "I don't know. I think Carol isn't thinking straight because of the tragedy she's just suffered."

Chapter Six

WHEN WE LEFT CAROL'S house, we headed back to Stormy's to talk to Natalie. I didn't believe for one minute that she could have done what Carol said she did back in the ninth grade. And the more I thought about it, the more it bothered me that she had even brought it up. What difference did it make at this point?

Before I got to Stormy's, I realized the reason it bothered me was that Carol had been stewing over who had killed Chrissy. I didn't want anyone looking at Natalie. Natalie wasn't capable of murder. I took a deep breath and reminded myself that Carol was dealing with a personal nightmare at that moment and her thinking wasn't clear.

"Natalie," Stormy said striding into the kitchen. Natalie was pouring cereal into a bowl. "Is it true you sabotaged Chrissy's science project in the ninth grade?"

Natalie looked at both of us, her forehead wrinkled in confusion. "No. Jenna Dennison did that. Chrissy stole her boyfriend and Jenna was furious. She wrote some nasty things about Chrissy on the poster board she had made for her project. I told you that."

I took a deep breath. "Why would Chrissy's mother think you were the one that did it?"

She shrugged and a distinctly guilty look crossed her face. "It was a long time ago. Jenna and I hung out for a while in the ninth grade. Maybe we both discussed it, but I had nothing to do with it."

"Did you get into trouble for it?" Stormy asked her.

She poured milk on her cereal and then picked up the bowl of cereal and took a bite, taking her time before answering us. "I did get blamed for it, but so did Jenna. We both received a failing grade for our project, but I never told you about it. It wasn't fair, but I didn't want to cause any problems so I didn't say anything. I just did some extra credit work and brought my grade back up." She shrugged and took another bite of her cereal.

I was suddenly feeling confused. First Natalie didn't want to go see Chrissy's parents to offer her condolences, and now she was saying that even though she was innocent of what had happened in the ninth grade, she silently suffered the consequences of what someone else had done.

"I can't believe you lied to me," Stormy said, crossing her arms in front of herself.

"I didn't lie to you. The subject never came up and besides that, it was five years ago. You're getting mad about something I did five years ago?"

"That's not the point," she said. "A girl is dead and you don't seem very concerned."

"Mom, I'm sorry Chrissy's dead. But it's not as if we'd been friends for years. I don't know who might have killed her, but like I said before, it was weird that she and Jenna teamed up."

Stormy took a deep breath. "Okay. You're right. It was a long time ago and there's no reason for me to get upset about it now." She glanced over at me.

"Where does Jenna work?" I asked Natalie.

"She works at the drugstore on Main Street."

STORMY AND I DROVE over to Sparrow drugs. The store was more deserted than I had expected with it being so close to Christmas. They had lots of cute gift items in the seasonal aisles and I decided I needed to come back and take a closer look when I wasn't on a mission. Right now, I had someone I needed to interview. Someone that might just be a suspect.

We found Jenna in the cosmetic department. There was a small sectioned off area where they kept the more expensive cosmetics locked up and she was back there straightening the displays of tester make up tubes and compacts.

"Hi Jenna," I said casually. "Congratulations on winning the gingerbread house decorating contest."

She turned around to look at me and smiled. "Thank you, Rainey," she said. "I was surprised we won. I thought Natalie did a really good job on your gingerbread house."

"We would have done better if the gingerbread house wasn't broken. I have a feeling you might know how that happened," I said. I was trying not to sound like I was accusing her and I hoped that came through in my tone.

She looked at me and bit her lower lip. "I guess I do. Chrissy broke your gingerbread house. I didn't know that for sure at first, but I suspected it. She got back before I did after the break and she was in our kitchenette, smiling smugly. Later while we were decorating, I asked her about it and she said she may have slipped into your kitchenette and accidentally bumped into it. She laughed about it. I thought it was a really rotten thing to do, but I had nothing to do with it."

I nodded. It didn't surprise me that Chrissy might have done something like that. "That was what I suspected," I said. "You didn't feel like you should mention it to the judges?"

She looked away and straightened up the tubes of lipstick in front of her. "I should have. But I was afraid of what Chrissy would do if I did. I couldn't bring myself to cross her. I'm sorry."

That wasn't a shock, either. I glanced at Stormy and rolled my eyes. "It was kind of a surprise to see you and Chrissy teaming up for the competition. I didn't know the two of you were such good friends."

Her eyes went wide. "We weren't. I was as surprised as anybody when Chrissy asked me to be her partner. She paid the entrance fee for me and that was the only reason I did it. I had always wanted to be in the competition, but I live on my own. I don't get paid a lot working here, so I couldn't afford it."

Jenna was a slightly built girl, but she was tall. Her strawberry blond hair complemented her pale complexion and her blue eyes were the color of ice. She was pretty in an unconventional way. "I was led to believe that you and Chrissy really hated each other when you were in school. In fact, someone may have said that you sabotaged her science class project."

"Somebody might have said you tried to blame it on someone else," Stormy interjected. Stormy was in mama bear mode at the moment, even though the situation had occurred years ago. I wondered if she felt someone might try to pin Chrissy's death on her daughter.

Jenna's eyes went from me to Stormy. "Natalie and I kidded and laughed about doing something like that. But we had no intention of carrying it through until Chrissy cornered me in the girl's bathroom and pushed my face into the sink. She had all of her friends behind her and there wasn't anything I could do. I got angry, and I did it. I sabotaged her project. When I told Mr. White what happened, you can bet he didn't believe me, and in my panic, I brought up Natalie's name. I hoped to have her back up my story so that maybe he would believe me because he really liked her. But we both ended up with failed projects."

Jenna seemed sincere in what she was saying although she was leaving out the part where Chrissy stole her boyfriend. "Do you have any idea what might have happened to Chrissy?"

She glanced over her shoulder and then looked at me again. "I really don't know. But Chrissy told me that Susan Lang, the organizer of the event, tried to keep her out of the competition."

"Why would she want to do that?" I asked. Susan was not only the organizer of the event, but she had been one of the judges for the competition.

"Chrissy said she didn't know why, but when she first tried to register, Susan told her they already had twelve teams and she was too late. Susan said that Tara Black and Kelly Ortega were the last team to register. Chrissy didn't believe her, so she went and asked Tara and Kelly when they had registered. Turns out we had submitted our registration form two days before they did and Chrissy went back and confronted Susan."

"What did Susan say?" I asked.

"I guess Susan didn't want to get caught in a lie, so she backed down and said another team had backed out and she let Chrissy and me in the competition. I think the truth was that there was still one more slot open, and she turned Chrissy down, hoping someone else would register. No one would know unless they asked around, and that's what Chrissy did."

"And Chrissy never mentioned why Susan didn't want her in the competition?" Stormy asked.

She shook her head. "No, I really don't know why. But I could tell when Susan was around us on the day of the competition, she didn't like Chrissy. I just figured Susan is a snooty person, and she was mad that Chrissy checked up on her. But I don't know why she didn't want us in the competition to begin with."

It sounded plausible. I didn't know Susan well, but I had always had the impression that she thought she was better than most people. She just had an air about her.

"When was last time you saw Chrissy?" I asked her.

"Right after the judging," she said. "I had to get to work, and I left around 4:15."

I nodded. "And you didn't speak to her again?"

She shook her head. "No. When I saw what she had done to your gingerbread house, I realized I had made a mistake teaming up with her. I got my trophy, and I left. I expected to never speak to her again, and I guess I was right, but not for the reasons I thought." She shrugged. "I didn't like Chrissy when we were in school, and I decided I didn't like her as an adult either."

I wasn't sure if everything Jenna said was the truth, but it was all I had for now.

Stormy and I left the drugstore without buying anything. I wondered what Susan Lang had against Chrissy. I agreed with Jenna though. Chrissy left a lot to be desired as a friend. She had gone out of her way to destroy our gingerbread house so she could win the contest. I had more questions than answers at this point, but I was going to find out who killed Chrissy Jones.

Chapter Seven

"ANOTHER MURDER?" AGATHA asked me. Agatha owned the British Coffee and Tea Company and had been a good friend of mine for years.

We were sitting in a corner booth at Sam's Diner and she was enjoying her breakfast. The weather had gotten colder with snow arriving overnight. The diner was nearly deserted, so I slid into the booth across from her to rest my feet for a few minutes.

I nodded. "It's a terrible shame. A murder this close to Christmas," I said. "Chrissy Jones."

"Chrissy Jones? Wasn't she that girl that worked over at Michelle's?" Agatha asked, eating a forkful of scrambled eggs. Michelle's was one of the nicest dress shops in Sparrow.

"Yes, I think she worked at Michelle's for a couple of years. She was a friend of Natalie's when they were young." I left out the part where they had had a nasty breakup and now Natalie was behaving slightly out of character regarding Chrissy's death.

She nodded. "That's what I thought. She was a beauty queen, wasn't she?"

"Yes, she was supposed to compete in the Miss America pageant, but from what I hear, she never made it."

"Those poor beauty queens," Agatha said and chuckled sadly. "They don't seem to be able to catch a break around here."

I nodded. "I hate the things that have happened around here lately. Did you know her?"

She shook her head. "Not really. She stopped in once in a while to get a coffee, and I shopped at Michelle's occasionally. But I wouldn't say that I really knew her. We exchanged pleasantries when we saw one another, but not much more than that."

"I just can't imagine who would want to kill her. I mean, she could be kind of arrogant sometimes," I said, remembering a conversation we had had several months earlier. Chrissy wasn't the shy type. She frequently bragged on herself. "But lots of people are arrogant and they don't end up dead."

She nodded. "I suppose some people are overly confident in themselves. Still, I feel bad for her parents. What a terrible loss."

"You can say that again," I said and looked up as Cade walked through the front door. He stopped and looked in our direction, then headed over to us.

"So, I've caught you lazing about, have I?" he said with a grin and sat next to me on the booth seat.

I scooted over to give him room. "I guess you have," I said and gave him a quick kiss. "Don't blame me though, blame the weather. It's too cold for people to venture out, even for Sam's cooking."

"I wouldn't be out here either if I didn't have to be," he said. He looked at Agatha's plate. "My Agatha, those scrambled eggs and white toast sure do look good."

"Is that a hint?" I asked.

"It could be," he said raising one eyebrow.

Cade was predictable where breakfast was concerned. He loved his scrambled eggs and white toast for breakfast. It made it simple and easy to remember. "I tell you what," I said. "You fill me in on what you know about Chrissy's death, and I'll go turn in an order to Sam for your scrambled eggs and toast."

He sat back in the seat and groaned. "You only want me around for my murder case information."

"Maybe. But maybe you know something that's useful," I said. "Spill it."

"Chrissy Jones died of blunt force trauma and we still don't know who did it," he said wickedly. "Does that satisfy you?"

"Hardly. I heard her gingerbread decorating partner, Jenna Dennison, hated her in school and yet they partnered for the contest. Kind of odd, eh?"

"Why would people who hate each other become partners?" he asked.

"According to Jenna, she always wanted to be in the competition and didn't have the entrance fee, so when Chrissy offered to pay, she jumped at the chance."

"Who wants to be in a gingerbread decorating contest bad enough to put up with someone that you hate?" he asked, suspiciously.

"That's what I thought. Kind of odd, if you ask me, but Jenna said Chrissy offered to pay the entrance fee because she was intent on winning, so that Natalie wouldn't."

"Why would that be important to her?" Agatha asked, a forkful of scrambled eggs poised midway to her mouth.

I looked at Agatha. "When I said Chrissy and Natalie had been friends, what I left out was that they had a terrible falling out in the seventh grade. Personally, I think Chrissy thought she was better than Natalie and dumped her when they got to junior high." I shrugged. "You know how hormonal girls are at that age."

"So Chrissy was still holding a grudge? But she was the instigator of the falling out?" she asked.

I nodded. "Natalie says she didn't have much to do with her after that, but apparently Chrissy still had some bad feelings toward Natalie."

"I see," she said. "There's no accounting for the actions of young girls sometimes."

"I sure could use a cup of coffee," Cade hinted.

I groaned. "You're going to make me get up, aren't you?"

He nodded. "That I am."

I playfully shoved him off the seat, and he got to his feet so I could get out of the booth and get him some coffee. Before I did that, I wrote down his breakfast order on a diner ticket and went into the kitchen to hand it to Sam.

"It's quiet out there isn't it?" Sam asked, turning from the grill.

I nodded. "You better believe it. But lucky for us, Cade just came through the door and ordered scrambled eggs and white toast."

Sam nodded. "That'll help me pay the rent," he said with a chuckle and went to get eggs from the refrigerator. "So what's up with the latest murder?"

I sighed. "I guess everyone knows I'm snooping around whenever there's a murder?"

"I don't know why you would even have to ask that. You know practically the whole town knows that."

"Sadly, I really don't know anything this time around. At least not yet. When I saw her under the table, there was blood coming from her head."

He returned to the griddle and began cracking eggs. "I'm sorry you had to see that."

I nodded. "I feel sorry for the young girl that found her. Poor thing. She looked like she was only sixteen or seventeen."

He shook his head. "It's a shame. I don't think I know anything about Chrissy Jones. That was her name, wasn't it?"

"Yes that was it. Something will turn up," I said and headed back out to get Cade a cup of coffee.

"I just made a new pot of coffee," Luanne said to me. She was standing at the coffee maker, waiting for the coffee to finish brewing. "I heard about Chrissy Jones."

"What did you hear?" I asked and got a cup from the cupboard for Cade.

"She lied about being in the competition for Miss America. Apparently, she couldn't qualify, but she told everybody she just didn't want to compete anymore."

I looked at her. "Why would she lie about that?"

Luanne shrugged. "Pride?"

"I guess that would do it, wouldn't it?" I said, thinking about this. "When I spoke to her a few months ago, she was feeling very sure of herself. She said she just knew she was going to win. Who did she tell that she didn't want to compete anymore?"

"She told me. But Chrissy's mother told me she didn't qualify. I saw her mother at Michelle's when I was shopping for a new dress right before Thanksgiving."

That was odd. Carol hadn't mentioned to Stormy and me that Chrissy had changed her mind about being in the Miss America pageant. She had said she never got a chance to compete, but she didn't say she hadn't qualified. "How well do you know Carol Jones?"

"She's my mother's second cousin," Luanne said nodding. "We don't talk to that side of the family very much, except when we do. When I ran into Carol, I asked her how Chrissy was and if we'd be seeing her on TV on the Miss America pageant next year. She said Chrissy didn't qualify, and she asked me not to tell anybody." Luanne turned to me and gasped. "Oh. I told somebody. But don't you tell anyone else, okay?"

Luanne wasn't trying to be cute. She was an airhead. "That's okay Luanne, I hardly tell anybody anything anyway."

She nodded. "I guess it's okay then. After Carol left the shop, Chrissy rang up the dress I had picked out, and she told me she didn't want to be in the Miss America pageant anymore. I thought it was weird since her mother just told me she didn't qualify, but I didn't tell her that." She turned and poured coffee into the cup I had brought over. "Is this for Cade?"

"It sure is," I said.

"Well you tell him I appreciate the hard work he does for this community."

I smiled. "That's very sweet of you, Luanne," I said. "But he's right at the corner booth with Agatha. You can just walk over there and tell him yourself if you want to."

"Oh no, I don't want to disturb him." She poured a cup of coffee for the one other customer in the diner and took it over to him.

I wasn't sure if what Luanne said was important to the case or not. I was going to have to dig deeper into this. I wondered if Carol would tell me anything if I asked her about Chrissy not qualifying the pageant. It did seem odd that Chrissy hadn't qualified. She had been in pageants since before she could walk and was as poised and perfected as any beauty queen I had ever met.

I headed back to the booth with Cade's coffee and set it in front of him. "Here you go."

"Well, Rainey, as much as I have enjoyed talking to you and your man here, I had better get back to work," Agatha said and got to her feet. "I'll talk to you all later."

"Bye, Agatha," I said as she headed to the cash register to pay. Luanne took her payment, and I slid into the booth across from Cade. "Details?"

He chuckled and took a sip of his coffee. "There was a bloody brick beneath the table where Chrissy was laying."

I inhaled. "How awful."

He nodded. "It is. I've talked to her parents, but they have no idea what might have happened. She came home after the gingerbread house contest but then went out with friends shortly afterward. Her mother said it wasn't unusual for her not to come home for a day or two and wasn't worried when she didn't."

"Stormy and I stopped by to tell Carol how sorry we were about Chrissy's death. She didn't have a lot to say, other than she thought it was suspicious that she partnered with Jenna Dennison. She did bring up the fact that Chrissy couldn't stand Natalie." I shrugged. "Hopefully you'll get a break in the case soon."

"Order up, Rainey!" I heard Sam call through the pass-through window.

"I'll be right back with your breakfast," I told him.

Getting hit in the head with a brick was a terrible way to die. It made me sad for Chrissy. She might not have been the nicest person around, but she didn't deserve to die that way.

Chapter Eight

IT WAS THE FOLLOWING afternoon when I ran into Susan Lang at the grocery store. She was looking over the bags of fresh cranberries in the produce department and I pushed my shopping cart next to hers.

"Hi Susan," I said. "Those cranberries look good, don't they?"

She turned to look at me and smiled back. "Hi Rainey," she said. "They do look good. I thought I'd better grab some before the season is over. I sure do love them."

I nodded. "I do too. It's convenient having the dried kind, but I prefer the fresh ones. As a matter of fact, I was thinking about picking up a bag or two along with some apples and making a cranberry apple pie."

She brightened at the mention of the cranberry apple pie. "That sounds really good. You have great ideas," she said. "I might do the same. I heard you were writing a cookbook, how's that coming?"

"It's going really well. I've been working on new recipes for several months now. I'm hoping to be done with the cookbook early next year," I said and chuckled. "It sounds like that's a long way off when I say 'early next year.'"

She smiled and put a bag of cranberries into her shopping cart. "It feels like this year went so fast."

I nodded. "Susan, can I ask you a question about the gingerbread house contest?"

One eyebrow arched upward. "Sure, what did you want to ask?"

"How is it handled? I heard that entering the contest is first-come first-served."

She looked away as she picked up another bag of cranberries. "That's exactly how it's done. If a team has the money to enter, and they get in before the slots are filled up, then they'll be accepted." She tilted her head and looked at me. "You know Rainey, there wasn't anything we could do about your broken gingerbread house. The rules specifically state that if something happens to the gingerbread house during the competition, it is the contestants' responsibility to fix it or bow out."

"I understand completely," I said, nodding. "But I have a question about Chrissy Jones and Jenna Dennison. When did they turn in their application?"

Her eyes narrowed. "If I remember right, they turned it in the first week of November. But I'd have to check my records to be sure. Why do you ask?"

"Then why didn't you want them in the competition?" I said, ignoring her question. I thought I might as well put it out there and see what she said.

She inhaled sharply and her body tensed up. "That's ridiculous. Who said I didn't want them in the competition? All they had to do was apply in time and have the entrance fee."

I shrugged. "I don't really remember who said it. I guess it's just a rumor going around. You know how it is around here."

She narrowed her eyes at me. "Well. It's an unfounded rumor. I didn't try to keep them out of the contest, and like I said, there wasn't anything we could do about your broken gingerbread house."

"Of course not. I understand completely. They created an absolutely beautiful gingerbread house and it deserved to win. Jenna is a very talented decorator." I left out the part where I thought that had ours not broken and looked a bit Frankenstein-ish, that we would have easily taken first place.

She gave me a curt nod of her head. "Good. As long as you understand there was nothing personal about it."

"No, I understand completely." I wasn't sure I believed what she said about not having an issue with Chrissy and Jenna being in the contest. I can't say exactly why, but maybe it was because she sounded defensive.

"How is the murder investigation going? I'm assuming that you know what's going on?" She tilted her head and smirked.

I shrugged, trying not to let on that I realized the question was meant to be catty. "I hear things occasionally, but it seems this one really is a mystery," I said. "I know Cade is working night and day on it and he'll have the killer behind bars before you know it."

"If you ask me," she said, and glanced over her shoulder. "And I know you didn't, but I'm going to say it anyway. You might want to talk to Elaine Jeffers and see what she knows about Chrissy's death." She gave me another smirk. Susan Lang could be snobby when she wanted to be.

"Elaine Jeffers? Doesn't she work at Michelle's dress shop?" I knew Elaine well enough to say hello to her and ask how she was.

She nodded and set the second bag of cranberries into the front of her shopping cart and turned back to the display of cranberries. "She sure does. And between you and me, and the bags of cranberries," she said and picked up another bag of cranberries. "She and Chrissy didn't get along. Chrissy accused her of stealing jewelry from the shop."

"Really?" This was news to me. "Did she do it?"

"I have no idea, but if you knew Elaine Jeffers, I think you'd have to say there's a very good possibility that she's guilty."

I considered this. "How do you know this?"

"My friend Michelle Watkins owns Michelle's. She told me she'd been having trouble with the two of them when they worked together and Chrissy said she saw Elaine steal a ring and a bracelet."

"Did she fire Elaine? I thought I saw her working there not long ago," I said and reached for a bag of cranberries. I held them up and looked them over to make sure none of them were mushy, and then tossed it into my cart.

"She said she couldn't because she had no proof. When Michelle confronted her, Elaine became livid. She swore up and down that she would never steal from anyone."

"But Michelle doesn't believe her?" I asked, picking up a small box of blackberries that were next to the cranberries and looking them over.

"Michelle has been looking for a reason to get rid of Elaine for months now. She had hoped that this was her chance, but there was no proof that she had taken anything. The ring and bracelet did disappear, but the day they were noticed was a day that Elaine didn't work, and she insisted she had nothing to do with it. Of course, Michelle thinks she took it the day before."

"If she's been trying to get rid of her for months, why doesn't she just do it?" I asked.

"Because Elaine threatened to take her to the board of labor and file a complaint against her for not allowing the girls to take their breaks. She doesn't want to get into a legal mess, so she's waiting until she has an ironclad reason to fire her. But, you didn't hear that from me and I would appreciate it if you would keep it quiet," she said leaning on her shopping cart.

I nodded. "It wouldn't be good to let something like that out. Tell me, Susan, do you know Elaine well?"

"I know her well enough to know that she's shady. She worked for Celia Markson at her flower shop when it was open. Celia caught her stealing and fired her a couple of years ago. Honestly, I warned Michelle about hiring her, but she thought she was doing a good deed for someone less fortunate. You know how those do-gooders are," she said and rolled her eyes.

Celia had owned the Perfect Florist Shop before she died last spring. "It would be a shame if Elaine hadn't learned her lesson the first time and stole from her new employer, but I guess it isn't that much of a stretch, is it?"

She shook her head. "No, it isn't. But things got worse when she found out that Chrissy was the one who accused her of stealing the necklace."

"How did she find out that Chrissy had accused her? Isn't that something Michelle would keep to herself?"

"Michelle did keep it to herself. But you know how Chrissy was. She was smug and full of herself. She told Elaine she had told Michelle she was stealing."

"That's crazy," I said. "Why on earth would Chrissy tell her that?"

She shrugged. "Like I said, Chrissy was smug and full of herself. I guess she thought there was nothing Elaine could do to her. But, I think there was something Elaine could do. And I think she did it and now Chrissy isn't going to be smug about anything anymore."

I considered this a moment. "If this was a funny situation, I'd say the joke was on Chrissy. But there's nothing funny about murder."

"You can say that again," she said. "I think you should stop in and speak to Elaine. Or at least tell Detective Starkey what I said. Michelle will back me up as long as it doesn't get around town. She doesn't want her business broadcast to everyone."

"I'll certainly let Cade know. I know he wants to get this case closed as soon as possible. It will be a relief to Chrissy's family to have the killer behind bars."

She nodded. "I'm sure they'll be relieved when that happens. It's just a shame that Chrissy couldn't keep her mouth shut. It wouldn't surprise me a bit if she's responsible for her own death because she couldn't be nice to someone."

"I guess that's a possibility," I agreed.

It was hard to believe Chrissy could be so dumb as to tell Elaine that she had told their boss she was stealing from the store, but people had done dumber things.

"It's been nice talking to you, Rainey," Susan said as she pushed her shopping cart toward the display of lettuce and salads. "Keep me in the loop if you hear anything interesting."

I wasn't going to keep her in the loop about anything. I wasn't entirely sure that anything she had said was true. If Michelle corroborated what she said, then I'd believe it. But even if she did, it still didn't mean that Susan might not have had something to do with Chrissy's death. I didn't think she was telling the truth about not trying to keep Chrissy and Jenna out of the Gingerbread house contest.

I picked up another bag of cranberries and put it into my cart and headed over to the display of apples. They had big shiny green Granny Smith apples on sale and I pulled a plastic bag from the roller near the corner of the apple display. An apple cranberry pie would be wonderful with cinnamon, butter, and brown sugar to sweeten it with. I was going to make Cade's sweet tooth a happy camper.

Chapter Nine

"THIS ISN'T WHAT I HAD in mind on a cold evening," Cade said as we walked along Blake Street.

"Oh? What did you have in mind?" I asked. My arm was looped through his and I walked as close to him as I could manage so I could borrow some of his warmth. It was cold out, and while a lot of the snow had melted, there was a light breeze that felt icy against my skin. I looked up at the stars twinkling in the ink-colored sky. It was a beautiful winter evening.

"Snuggling up in front of the fireplace next to you," he said. "Or, you know, hanging out someplace where it's nice and warm and were my face won't freeze off."

"Look on the bright side, we're out here enjoying the Christmas season," I said and sniffled. "When we finish up here, I'll rub your face until it's warm again."

"Of course that's the bright side," he said. "But what are you going to do if my nose freezes off my face?"

"I'll glue it back on. Don't you worry about a thing," I said and winked at him. "I've got a plan for everything."

We had joined a group of community Christmas carolers and were currently making the rounds of the area around the

Center Plaza fountain. I was only a mediocre singer, but I had missed doing this when I lived in New York and I wasn't going to let my first Christmas back home in Sparrow be without caroling.

"As you wish, Miss," he said, in his incredibly bad British accent. He usually saved it for moments like this.

I chuckled. He knew it was bad, but that didn't stop him. That's one of the things I liked about him. He wasn't afraid to be goofy with me.

As the choir started singing *O come all ye faithful*, we followed along near the back of the group and sang along. Or I should say, I sang. Cade was silent as we walked and I wondered if he was just shy, or if he really couldn't sing.

I elbowed him and when he turned to look at me, I said, "sing!"

He rolled his eyes and when the chorus started, he joined in. I turned and stared at him. Cade had a beautiful, rich baritone voice. He shrugged and tried to suppress a smile as I stared at him open-mouthed.

The shop fronts were beautiful with their Christmas decorations. Most of the windows were framed in Christmas lights and each storefront was done up with different Christmas themes. My favorite was the toy store that had vintage toys in the window along with an old train set that ran around a lake. Along the train tracks were cozy Christmas cottages and scattered around were toys from the early nineteenth and twentieth centuries.

We sang for over an hour, and when we were done, we stopped off at the corner coffee shop and ran inside. The warmth of the coffee shop made me giddy. I had begun to lose feeling in my face and my toes and it was a welcome respite from the cold.

"Wow," I said to Cade. "It feels so good in here!"

"I told you it would have been better if we stayed home in front of the fireplace," he said as we got into the line at the counter.

"No, this was an experience that we will never forget. Forty years from now, you'll say, remember when we spent our first Christmas together caroling along Blake Street?"

He eyed me and grinned. "I bet I will be saying that in forty years."

The impact of his words hit me, and I looked away. I had thought I had lost all chance of finding real love when my former husband and I divorced. To think about spending forty years with Cade was more than a dream come true. It felt like too much to ask for.

"I think I'm going to get a cup of hot cocoa," I said looking over the menu on the wall.

"Cocoa sounds good," he agreed quietly. "And look, they have those giant marshmallows to put in it if you want one."

I nodded. "That's the best part of getting cocoa from this shop." I felt like I had just put a damper on the evening by avoiding the subject of us being together for a long time, but I didn't know how to recover the lightheartedness we had had. I wanted to be with Cade more than anything, but I was afraid I would mess it up somehow.

The line moved quickly, and we placed our order. "Do you want to sit in here for a little while?" he asked me.

I nodded. "Yes, I want to finish warming up before we go back outside."

"You want to warm up before you get frozen again?" he asked, teasing.

I smiled at him. "I do. Staying cold all the time isn't any fun," I said, and we headed to a corner table and sat down. The warm cup of cocoa felt good in my hands.

"Sparrow is turning out to be a nice little town," he said as we sat down. "I'm glad I moved here."

I nodded. "I missed it when I lived in New York. I'm glad I came back. And I'm glad you moved here, too," I said, feeling like I was probably adding to the awkwardness of the situation.

He grinned. "Great cocoa." He held his cup up and then took another sip.

I nodded. "Do you know anything new about Chrissy's death?"

"Not a lot," he said lowering his voice. "I think I forgot to tell you that there was a cake decorating kit beneath the table where we found Chrissy's body."

I looked at him. "A cake decorating kit? I guess when they moved the gingerbread houses over, one of the winners could have brought it along in case the frosting got damaged."

He shrugged. "Could be. If you get some time, can you come down to the station and take a look at it? Maybe you'll remember if it belonged to Chrissy or her partner."

I nodded. "I can do that. I'm not really sure I remember what they used though. How long do you think she was under that table?"

"Probably all day. There were volunteers in the workshop and customers at the nearby shops, so she probably was killed the night before," he said and took a sip of his cocoa.

"So the killer probably had a key to Santa's workshop," I surmised. I made a mental note to find out who had access to the workshop.

The front door of the coffee shop swung open and Jenna Dennison walked in with Ryan Sparks. They were arm in arm, giggling and laughing about something as they walked up to the front counter to place their order.

"I think we know that guy from somewhere," Cade said as he followed my gaze.

I nodded. "We sure do. If you'll recall, a few months ago I felt very strongly that he might have killed Chrissy's rival, Pamela North."

"He did have a flimsy story," he said, keeping his eyes on Ryan.

"Flimsy is right. But, he was innocent. That time," I said giving Cade a sly look. "I wonder when he last saw Chrissy?"

He chuckled. "I bet if it was recently you'll find out, and he'll be sorry that you did."

I shrugged and laughed. "If I have to speak to him about another dead beauty queen, you can bet he's going to be sorry." Poor Ryan thought I wasn't very nice the last time I had talked to him, and if he became a suspect in another murder, I was going to let him have it. It wasn't that I was mean. I was just persistent.

"You should stay away from possible killers," he said mildly.

"Why? I've been a great help to you," I pointed out. "Besides, it's not like anything bad has ever happened."

"Oh?" he said. "I seem to recall you nearly getting your head blown off recently."

I hesitated. "Okay, maybe I should be more careful then," I agreed. I didn't want another situation like that on my hands and I reminded myself that I had made a decision to not accuse anyone of murder anymore.

"That's Chrissy's gingerbread house decorating partner with him, isn't it?" he asked, returning his gaze to the couple at the counter.

"Yes it is," I said. "I have my suspicions about her."

"Why doesn't that surprise me? What about him? Are you suspicious of him too?"

"I don't know yet," I said. "But I might be. Especially if he hangs around Jenna much."

"Just leave the investigating to me," he said and took another drink of his cocoa. "My marshmallow is nice and melty."

I chuckled. "I'm so glad to hear it," I said. "It's kind of odd that those two are together. I mean, especially since he was with Pamela North before she died."

"I thought I arrested Pamela North's killer?" he asked pointedly.

"Stop it. Of course you arrested her killer. Still, it seems odd." I took a sip of my cocoa.

"Small towns are full of odd people," he teased.

"I guess you can say that," I returned, rolling my eyes. "Everybody knows everybody and everyone knows everyone else's business. It's not one of the bonuses of living in a small town."

"You know what I'm wondering?" he asked me.

"What?"

"If that decorating kit belonged to Jenna."

"That's a really good question," I said. I hadn't really paid attention to what kind of decorating set Jenna had used, but maybe if I saw the one Cade had recovered it would trigger my memory. "I want to see that kit."

He nodded. "Why don't you stop by the station tomorrow and I'll show it to you?"

"That sounds like a plan," I said.

Jenna and Ryan got their drink orders and left the shop without ever looking in our direction. I wasn't sure if that was on purpose or they just hadn't noticed anyone around them. They seemed very involved with one another.

I turned back to him. Cade had finished sanding and refinishing my hardwood floors in my new house, and then he had helped me hang lights on the outside and put up my Christmas tree. I'd never had someone do anything like that for me. My ex-husband wasn't very hands-on with anything. He preferred to hire out manual labor.

"You know what I want to do?" he asked me.

I shook my head. "What?"

"I want to build a snowman." He grinned at me.

"It's too cold to build a snowman tonight," I said to him. "Besides, most of the snow has melted and what's left is kind of dirty."

"I didn't mean tonight. But when we get the next really good snow, let's build a snowman in your front yard."

"With a carrot for a nose and coal for his eyes and buttons?"

"I wouldn't have it any other way," he said.

I sighed. This was shaping up to be perhaps the best Christmas I'd ever had.

Chapter Ten

THE NEXT MORNING I went to Michelle's to see if Elaine was around. I needed to finish up Christmas shopping anyway, so I had a good excuse to stop in.

The dress shop window was decorated with adorable Christmas dresses and outfits as well as some that were a little dressier for New Year's Eve. I stepped inside the warm, cozy store. There were three other customers looking through racks of clothing and I spotted Elaine hanging up dresses near the back of the shop.

I made my way back to where she was working, hoping it didn't seem like I was headed back there to talk to her specifically. I stopped at a rack of red sweaters and picked one up. They were cashmere and felt wonderfully soft. I wondered if Stormy would like one for Christmas, but I had already spent a lot of money on the snow globe she had spotted at the gift shop and a couple of other items. I hung the sweater back up and moved over to where Elaine was.

"That dress sure is pretty," I said looking at the one she held in her hand.

She turned and smiled at me. "Isn't it though? I've been thinking I needed a new Christmas dress," she said and laughed. "I'll use any excuse to buy a new dress."

"I know what you mean, that's why I'm here. It's Christmas and I've got to have something nice to wear," I agreed. "I bet it's hard working here. Michelle's carries such cute clothes. I think I'd spend my entire paycheck on clothes if I worked here."

She nodded. "You have no idea. I think I've spent more money on clothes since I've worked here this past year than I have in my entire life."

I chuckled. "I can totally see that happening."

"Would you like to try it on?" she asked me, holding up the dress.

"I better not. I need to keep my mind focused on buying gifts for Christmas. Otherwise I'll spend more money than my budget allows for."

"You're a smart one, Rainey," she said. "I could learn a lot from you. I've already blown my last paycheck on clothes."

"So are you enjoying the seasonal events, Elaine? I went Caroling last night with my boyfriend and Natalie and I entered the gingerbread house contest."

"I have. I've been volunteering at Santa's workshop. I got to be an elf twice and a couple of other times I got to sell toys and gifts. It's been fun," she beamed.

I had to restrain myself from saying, *aha!* She had access to Santa's workshop.

"I sure was sorry to hear what happened to your coworker, Chrissy Jones," I said.

She looked at me, the smile slipping from her face. "It was a terrible tragedy, wasn't it? It's hard to believe she's gone."

I nodded. "Chrissy and my niece were friends when they were kids. When I come in here to shop, Chrissy was always so helpful."

Her jaw tightened. "She was helpful, wasn't she?" she said sounding noncommittal and turning to the rack to hang the dress up.

"It's a shame it happened so close to Christmas," I continued. "Someone dying so young is always terrible, but it seems worse because it happened this time of year." I was hoping she would open up if I kept talking.

"It is a shame it happened so near the holiday," she agreed without looking at me. "Her poor family will always be reminded of her death every Christmas."

"I don't know what I'd do if one of my family members died during the holidays," I said. "Don't you know my niece, Natalie?"

She nodded. "Yes, I know Natalie. I was a couple of years ahead of her in school. But we weren't close or anything. We ran in different circles."

"She's home from college for the holidays. I'm surprised she hasn't stopped in to do some Christmas shopping. Of course, that girl loves clothes, so maybe it's good she hasn't stopped in." I laughed. "She might spend all her money on clothes for herself."

"She still has some time if she still needs to do some Christmas shopping," she said. "Have you heard anything about who killed Chrissy?" She glanced at me as she hung another dress on the rack.

"Not really. All I know is that the police are investigating. I can't imagine how anyone could kill another human being." I shook my head while keeping one eye on her.

She hesitated, and glanced at me, and then went back to hanging dresses on the rack. "Me either," she finally said. "I guess some people have no ethics. I heard she was hit on the head." She glanced at me again for confirmation.

"Yes, she died from blunt force trauma. I was shopping nearby when a teenaged girl found her. Poor girl was traumatized," I said picking up another dress from the rack. This one had sparkles on the top and the skirt flowed out. It would make a lovely party dress. I turned over the price tag and almost choked. I hadn't paid that much for a dress since I lived in New York City and was attending the book release parties that my publisher held. I hung the dress back up. It would have to wait.

"Somehow I think blunt force trauma makes it worse," she said. "Don't you? Someone had to get up close and personal with her in order to do that. How could they look her in the face and kill her?"

I looked at her. "That's true. I thought the same thing." I was still trying to get the vision of her lying beneath the table out of my mind.

"What a shame," she murmured, looking away.

"I'm sure you're going to miss working with Chrissy, aren't you?" I said.

She looked at me and her mouth formed a hard line. "Not really. Chrissy wasn't exactly a gem to work with, if you want to know the truth."

"I'm sorry to hear that," I said. "It can be hard working with someone you don't particularly care for."

"That's the truth. I told our boss that Chrissy was nothing but trouble. She was always gossiping about other employees and trying to get people to fight with one another," she said as she hung up another dress. She missed the hook, and it slipped to the floor. When she bent over and picked it up, her cheeks had turned pink.

"I hate working with people like that," I said. "I've had more than my share of people I've worked with that I didn't particularly like. It makes the work day much longer, doesn't it?"

"It sure does. But Michelle didn't care. For some reason she really liked Chrissy, and I never could figure out why. As soon as she would leave the shop, Chrissy would say awful things about her," she snorted. "But I guess since she never heard any of it, or she would have known how Chrissy really felt about her."

I made a clucking sound. "Some people are easily fooled." I picked up a red dress. This one wasn't as fancy as the black one, but it was deep red and I really liked it.

"You can say that again," she said and chuckled. "Every time she walked in the room, Chrissy was flattering her. Telling her what great taste she had when she picked out clothes to sell here in the store, and how pretty she looked that day." Elaine shook her head. "It never ended."

"She does have really nice things in the store though," I said. "You have to admit that."

"Yes, but the truth is that I help her to pick things out. She's always asking me for my opinion on fashion, but I never get any credit for anything around here."

Elaine's cheeks had turned a darker pink as she huffed air through her mouth.

"That's frustrating," I said. "I don't understand why some people don't give proper credit when someone has done a great job at work. But at least now you won't have to deal with Chrissy anymore." I hung the red dress up again and looked at her. "I'm sorry. That was uncalled for."

"No, it's completely accurate. I won't have to deal with Chrissy anymore," she said. Then she looked at me. "And neither will Natalie."

I stopped, my hand on another dress that I had been ready to pick up. "What do you mean, neither will Natalie?"

She shrugged. "Natalie never got along with Chrissy after they had that big fight back in the seventh grade. Natalie hated Chrissy."

I didn't like the direction this conversation was going. Natalie had left the trouble she had had with Chrissy behind her years ago. "Natalie doesn't even mention Chrissy anymore. I doubt she has any issues with her."

She looked at me, one eyebrow raised. "Doesn't she? Because I saw her at the fountain earlier on the day Chrissy's body was found. She seemed really happy."

My heart stopped for a moment, and when it resumed beating it slammed into the wall of my chest. "What do you mean? What do you mean you saw her at the fountain?"

She shrugged. "She was hanging out down there by herself. When I heard Chrissy was dead, I just figured Natalie had finally had enough, and she handled her problems once and for all."

"I don't know what you're trying to suggest, Elaine," I said. I could feel the anger rising inside of me. "Natalie would never harm a fly. She's been over their broken friendship for years."

She shrugged as a small smile played on her lips. "Okay. If that's the way it is, then that's the way it is. Maybe I'm jumping to conclusions. I'm just saying I saw her down there. She and Chrissy had an argument two days before the gingerbread house contest and I just figured Natalie was pushed beyond her limits. I don't blame her. Chrissy was a hateful person."

My mouth went dry as my mind scrambled to process this. Natalie had gone home after the gingerbread house contest. She had been disheartened over the broken gingerbread house and the fact that we came in fourth place. Stormy had said Natalie was home that evening and had hung around the house the next day until we went shopping that night.

"What did they argue about?" I asked, finally getting my mouth to work.

She shrugged. "I don't really know," she said. "Something about a boy. Chrissy said she would get even with her, but maybe whatever she had planned backfired on her."

Chapter Eleven

I WAS SHAKING WHEN I pulled up to Stormy's house. I was supposed to be at the diner in less than half an hour, but I didn't care. I needed to speak with Natalie. I was sure Elaine had to be a wrong about Natalie being at the fountain the day Chrissy was found. Stormy had told me she was at home, but it was possible she had mixed up the days and wasn't remembering right. I was grasping at straws, and I told myself Natalie would have a plausible explanation.

I pounded harder on Stormy's door than I intended. When no one came to the door immediately, I tried the doorknob and found it unlocked. I pushed open the door and walked into the house uninvited. We were sisters after all, and I told myself it would be fine.

"Hi Rainey," Stormy said coming out of the kitchen wiping her hands on a dishtowel. "I was just washing my hands and couldn't get to the door when you knocked. What's going on?"

I stopped and tried to catch my breath. "Is Natalie here?"

Her eyebrows furrowed. "Is everything okay?"

I nodded. "Yes, where's Natalie?"

"She's in her room. What's going on, Rainey?"

"I just need to speak to her," I said and headed down the hall to Natalie's room. The door was open a crack, and I pushed it open without knocking.

Natalie looked at me from where she lay on her bed. She had been reading a book, and she looked surprised to see me. "Aunt Rainey," she said hesitantly. "Hi."

I nodded again, the movement of my head was exaggerated in my anxiety. Because that was what I was feeling. Anxiety. "Natalie," I said and stopped. How did I ask my niece if she was a murderer?

Her eyes went to her mother and then back to me. "Aunt Rainey, is everything okay?"

I stopped myself from nodding in that exaggerated manner again. "Natalie, did you have an argument with Chrissy a couple of days before the gingerbread decorating contest?"

Her face went blank. "I guess you could call it an argument," she said slowly. "But it wasn't really. It was just Chrissy being Chrissy."

"What does that mean?" I asked.

"Rainey, what's going on?" Stormy asked me. She had been standing in the doorway and now she walked into the bedroom and stood beside me.

"What does Chrissy being Chrissy mean?" I asked Natalie, ignoring Stormy's question.

She shrugged. "Chrissy thought the world revolved around her. You know how she was. It was one of the reasons we stopped being friends years ago. I just couldn't take being made feel like I was second best, so we ended our friendship. And when I registered for the contest, she made a comment about me not being good enough to win because I was never good enough for anything. I told her she might not think I was good enough, but I was going to win the contest. I know that's why she broke our gingerbread house. She knew we were going to win." She shook her head. "Things might have gotten a little heated, but it was nothing."

Hearing her say the argument didn't amount to anything calmed me. I was starting to feel like I had made a mistake, but I needed to hear it from her. "Did you argue about a boy?"

Her eyes went to Stormy and then back to me. "No, we didn't argue about a boy. Who would we argue about? I don't even live in Sparrow anymore."

I nodded again. "I see. And were you near the fountain on the day Chrissy's body was found?"

"Why are you asking me these things, Aunt Rainey?" Natalie said, sitting up on the side of the bed. "I think those are weird things to ask me."

"Rainey, what's going on here?" Stormy asked me.

I looked at Stormy. "I'm sure it's nothing. It's just that someone said something about Natalie arguing with Chrissy a couple of days before she died. I knew it didn't amount to much." I looked at Natalie for confirmation.

"You think I killed Chrissy?" she asked me.

I could see the hurt in her eyes and I wished I had a hole to crawl into. Natalie couldn't have hurt anyone. I shook my head. "No, I know you couldn't kill anyone, Natalie. It's just—I wanted to hear it from you."

She got to her feet as tears sprang to her eyes. "Aunt Rainey, I just can't believe you would even ask me that. I couldn't kill anyone. How could you think that of me?"

"I know," I said. "I'm being ridiculous. I knew it was stupid to even ask you about it. I'm sorry." I suddenly felt like an idiot. Natalie was one of the sweetest people I knew and she couldn't have killed anyone.

"Aunt Rainey, I have never been so insulted in all my life," she said, her cheeks turning red. "How could you even think this?"

"Natalie, I'm so sorry," I said. "I know it's stupid. I was an idiot for even coming here and asking you about it. I'm so sorry."

"Natalie was here all day after she got back from the gingerbread house judging contest until we went shopping the next evening. Weren't you Natalie?" Stormy asked. "I think I told you that, Rainey."

Natalie's eyes went to Stormy. "No," she said and looked away. "I volunteered to be an elf at Santa's workshop the morning after the gingerbread decorating contest. I just can't believe anybody would even think I would do something like that."

My heart sank when she admitted to being at Santa's workshop the morning Chrissy died. "How long were you there?"

She shrugged. "Two hours. Why? Why are you asking me these things?"

"You know your Aunt Rainey doesn't mean anything by it, Natalie," Stormy said. "She's just trying to help Cade figure out what happened to Chrissy. If Chrissy had still been your best friend, you would have expected her to help out."

She sighed, but looked away from me. "I guess you're right," she said and sat back down on the edge of the bed. "I don't feel good about Chrissy being killed, you know. We may not have gotten along in years, but I wouldn't wish death on her or anyone else."

"I know that," I said, still feeling sick over what I had done. I had allowed panic to take over and hurt her without thinking. "I'm sorry Natalie."

She nodded, but still didn't look at me. "It's fine."

I looked at Stormy helplessly. She gave me a slight nod of her head for reassurance. "I guess I better get to the diner," I said. "They're expecting me at work in a few minutes. Natalie, I really am sorry."

She nodded. "I know. I shouldn't have gotten so upset. I know you're just trying to help Cade."

I was relieved she wasn't going to hold it against me. "Well, I better get going," I said and left the room. Stormy followed behind me, and when we got outside, I stopped and turned to Stormy. "I'm sorry. I feel like an idiot."

"Don't feel like an idiot," Stormy said and gave me a quick hug. When she released me she asked, "But why did you ask her about it? I mean, did you really think she might have done it?"

"I spoke to Elaine Jeffers at Michelle's dress shop. She said she saw Natalie at the fountain the morning Chrissy's body was found. She said Chrissy and Natalie had argued a couple of days before the gingerbread house contest and she thought Natalie had finally had enough of Chrissy and killed her."

Stormy gasped. "She thought she got tired of Chrissy and killed her? Like people just get tired of people and kill them? And now Elaine is spreading that around?"

If I had stopped to think about it, I would have realized how ridiculous it all sounded. "She said Chrissy and Natalie hated each other and made it sound like they argued. On more than one occasion. But I always thought once they had had that falling out back in the seventh grade that they hadn't had anything to do with one another."

"I was under the same impression," Stormy said. "I can see where Chrissy might have been difficult to deal with. She was proud of herself, and maybe she was tormenting Natalie when they were still in school together. It wouldn't surprise me if Natalie never said anything about it."

I nodded. "I feel terrible for questioning her. I should have known better," I said.

"Don't beat yourself up for it," she said. "We all make mistakes and Natalie isn't one to hold a grudge."

That made me feel better, and I realized it was true. Natalie had never held a grudge against anyone. She wouldn't have even held a grudge against Chrissy for how she had treated her. I decided not to think about the fact that Natalie admitted to being at Santa's workshop the day Chrissy died. At least, I wouldn't think about it right now.

"I've got to get to work now," I said. "I'll talk to you later. Let me know if you think Natalie is upset about this whole thing. I'll find a way to make it up to her."

I got into my car and put my seatbelt on, stopping for a minute to take a deep breath. When I had settled down, I pulled away from the curb and headed to work.

Chapter Twelve

I WORKED MY SHIFT AT the diner still feeling guilty for having asked Natalie the questions I had. I knew our relationship would be fine, but in hindsight I realize how stupid it was.

When I finished up at the diner I headed over to the police station to meet Cade for an early dinner. It was just after three o'clock in the afternoon, but he wanted to show me the cake decorating kit that was found near Chrissy's body. Most cake decorating kits were fairly generic, but I thought I'd take a look anyway. It probably belonged to one of the contest winners and was left behind, then knocked off the table.

"Hey Rainey," Ted Wiese said when I walked through the doors of the police station. He was sitting at the front desk, his computer screen opened to Target.com. He toggled off as he greeted me and tried to shield his screen with his body.

"Hi Ted," I said, walking up to the front desk. "Getting some Christmas shopping done?"

He chuckled. "You caught me did you?"

I grinned. "Don't worry, I won't tell anyone. Is Cade around?"

"Sure, he's in his office," he said. "When are we going to get some Christmas cookies around here?"

I shrugged. "I don't know, depends on if Santa says you've been a good police officer or not."

"Well, I'm pretty sure I've been a very good police officer," he said and chuckled. "You can go on back and see Cade if you want."

"You know I want," I said and headed to the door that led down a hallway and to Cade's office.

I knocked on Cade's door and waited for him to answer.

"Come in," he called from the other side.

I pushed the door open and closed it behind me. "Hey," I said and went to his desk, leaned over and gave him a kiss. "How are you?"

"I'm doing just fine," he said. "How are you doing? I think that's the real question."

I looked at him. Had someone told him I had asked Natalie about killing Chrissy? I sat down. "What do you mean? I'm fine."

One eyebrow rose up as he looked at me questioningly. "What do you mean?"

I shrugged and chuckled. "I have no idea where we're going with this conversation," I said. "Where's that decorating kit?"

He grinned and turned around to the credenza behind him and picked it up, then turned around and set it on his desk. For the second time today, my heart stopped beating. The canvas tote bag had a floral print with ladybugs on it. It was Natalie's.

"You found this near Chrissy's body?" I asked and heard the tremor in my own voice.

He nodded. "Yup, it was on the floor next to her. Why?"

When my heart came back to life it slammed into my chest wall and I had to inhale deeply to get enough oxygen into my body.

"No reason," I said, trying to piece this together. There had to be a good explanation as to why it was at the crime scene. Our gingerbread house wasn't on display so there was no need to bring the decorating kit to Santa's workshop.

His brow furrowed. "I'd say by the look on your face, there is a reason. What's going on Rainey?" he asked. His eyes went to the bag and then back to me.

I stared at him for a moment before speaking. "It's Natalie's."

Now both eyebrows shot up. "Natalie's? Are you sure?"

I nodded slowly. "Yes, she brought it to the gingerbread house competition. We were joking about it being so cute," I said. "She decorated our gingerbread house with that kit."

He looked at it again. "Any idea why it would be near the body?"

I shook my head. "I have no idea. Maybe she loaned it to one of the winners in case they needed to touch up their gingerbread house." I might have been grasping at straws once again, but I was going to grasp until I had a chance to speak to Natalie again.

"I suppose that's possible," he said. "Do you know where Natalie bought hers from?"

"She said it was from a cake decorating supplier online. She was so excited about us teaming up to compete in this competition that she bought a lot of new decorating tips and other supplies and then bought the floral canvas bag to put them in." I pulled the bag to me and opened it, looking at the tips and other items in it. I couldn't tell if it was all there, but it looked like it was. I sat back in my chair, trying to think.

"Maybe you can ask to borrow her kit," he suggested. "See if she still has it. It's possible someone else had one just like it, isn't it?"

My eyes were on the bag on the desk in front of me. "No, not with that bag. I know that my niece did not kill anyone. She doesn't have it in her." I looked up at him.

"Of course not," he said. "Besides, maybe someone borrowed her kit and Natalie didn't notice it went missing."

I looked at him. "That is an absolutely brilliant thought," I said with relief. But Cade was a detective. He wasn't going to let it go at that and I wouldn't expect him to. If Natalie were missing her entire decorating kit, I was sure she would have mentioned it.

He sighed. "Do you know where Natalie was the day Chrissy was murdered?"

"She was at home," I said. "And, she said she volunteered as Santa's elf for a couple of hours that morning." I hated to admit that she was anywhere near the murder scene, but I couldn't lie about it.

"And she has an alibi? Someone that will agree that she was home most of the day? I'm assuming Santa will vouch for her while she was there at the workshop?" He gave me a grin to try and make me feel better.

"Stormy said she was home most of the day," I said. I sighed. "Cade, this is making me sick. I went and spoke to Elaine Jeffers at Michelle's dress shop today. She said Natalie and Chrissy had an argument a couple of days before the competition. Natalie admitted that she had words with Chrissy."

"I'm not going to ask if you think Natalie killed someone. You already said you don't think she could. And honestly, I think I know Natalie well enough to know that she isn't capable of murder. An argument doesn't necessarily mean anything."

I sat back in my chair. "I asked Natalie if anything happened between her and Chrissy," I said. "She said she and Chrissy argued, but denied that anything significant happened. I know she has to be telling the truth. She didn't do anything wrong."

He nodded. "I believe you."

"Then why do I feel so terrible about this whole thing? No, scared. I feel scared." I looked at him, hoping for reassurance that my imagination was running away with me.

"Someone is dead and somebody else pointed a finger at someone that you're very close to," he said mildly. "I think feeling a little worried is normal. Didn't you tell me that she and Chrissy were friends when they were younger?"

"Yes, they were best friends from the time they were toddlers until the seventh grade. But they had a big argument, and they ended their friendship."

"What was the argument over?" he asked me.

"Natalie has never gone into a lot of detail, but she did say she was tired of being made to feel like she wasn't as good as Chrissy. Chrissy thought she was better than other people. I think that might have come from being an only child. Her parents indulged her. I guess it just got to be too much for Natalie."

"How did Natalie feel when the friendship ended?" he asked me.

I sighed. "It broke her heart. They had been so close for most of their lives and I think it came as a shock to her. But that was a long time ago. She's been over it for years."

He nodded. "Natalie doesn't seem the type to hold a grudge. I've always had the impression that she's an even-tempered person."

"She really is. She has a lot of friends that care for her." I brushed the hair out of my face and sat back in my chair. "You don't suspect Natalie, do you?"

He looked at me soberly. "I'm going to stop by and talk to her. But don't think that means I'm suspicious of her or that I'm going to accuse her. I'd hate to see the two of you try to escape Sparrow and drive across the country. I don't think you'd do well being on the lam."

I chuckled. Cade always knew how to make me feel better. "Can't you just see it? If I thought for one minute you were going to arrest my niece, I'd steal her way and drive her to New York City where you'd never find us."

"You doubt my abilities as a detective? I bet I could track you down." He eyed me.

I considered this. "You could try, but you don't know who you're dealing with. A desperate aunt that's protecting her niece will defeat a determined detective any day."

He narrowed his eyes at me. "Don't think for a minute that I'd let you escape just because you're cute."

"I'm banking on the fact that you'd let me escape just because I'm cute," I said.

He chuckled. "It's early for dinner, but I only had time to eat a donut for lunch. Is it too early for you to eat?"

I shook my head. "It's never too early for me to eat. It's kind of a hobby of mine."

He got to his feet and tucked the decorating kit into a bottom desk drawer and locked it with a key. "Then let's go get something to eat."

"I'd suggest the diner, but it's closed. We need to find someplace that's nice and warm and serves soup." I said as we headed out the door of his office.

"Soup?" he said closing the door behind him. "You want soup?"

"I want something warm and filling," I said. "Potato soup or clam chowder. Something hearty with some homemade bread."

I was glad Cade wasn't seriously thinking that Natalie could be a murderer. If he had, I don't know if our relationship could handle it. No, that wasn't true. I was sure our relationship would be fine because there was no chance that Natalie had killed Chrissy Jones and he wouldn't accuse anyone without evidence they had committed a crime.

Chapter Thirteen

THE MORNING OF CHRISSY'S funeral was cold and overcast. It was a dreary day and in many ways, it was fitting. The little church was packed, and I squeezed into the back pew with Mom and Stormy. I wasn't surprised at the size of the small crowd that had showed up; Chrissy's family was one of the most prominent families in Sparrow. Her father was in real estate and her mother was manager of one of the banks in town. Chrissy had been featured in the newspaper on many occasions throughout her childhood because of the beauty pageants she had won. Sadly, she had been an only child which made her murder that much harder for her parents.

I had hoped Natalie would come along with us to the funeral, but she had refused. I wasn't sure what to make of that. If, like she said, she was over their former friendship and break up, why didn't she want to come to the funeral to pay her respects to Chrissy's parents? It didn't sit well with me. It seemed like the least she could do.

"Do you see anybody suspicious?" Mom whispered, glancing around the room.

"No, I doubt people are going to act suspicious at a funeral," I said.

"Murderers always give themselves away," Mom said. "They're just so suspicious looking. Pay attention."

"Well if that was true, then no one would get away with murder, would they?" I said, giving my mother the eye.

She shrugged. "Fine. Have it your way. But I'm still looking for suspicious people."

I glanced over at Stormy sitting next to me. She had been quiet since I picked her up. "How are you doing, sis?"

She turned and looked at me and I saw the tears that threatened to fall. "I just keep thinking, what if that were Natalie? I could never live through something like that."

I nodded. "I know what you mean. They may be your children, but those five little ones are the most important people in my life. And Cade, of course."

Mom reached across me and gave Stormy's knee a squeeze. "We'll all just be thankful that we still have one another."

I saw Cade slip into the back of the church and I nodded to him. He nodded back but made no effort to join us. I figured he would probably just stand in the back and watch the crowd. Chrissy's death had been violent and ugly, and I knew he wanted to find the killer as soon as possible.

I saw Carol's shoulders shake as she dropped her head. Roger put his arm around her and whispered something to her. I took a deep breath. Christmas would never be the same for them. Life would never be the same for them.

Jenna arrived, and I watched as she made her way down the aisle to pay her final respects. I thought it was odd, given what both she and Natalie had told me about their relationship. I watched her as she put both hands on the side of the casket and looked in at Chrissy. I couldn't bear to go and look at Chrissy myself. I decided I was going to skip it this time around.

"Is that the killer?" Mom whispered, leaning toward me.

I turned to her and gave her a deadpan look. "Really, Mom?"

She shrugged. "I'm just trying to help."

The pastor took the podium and began the service. I was going to figure out who killed Chrissy, if only to clear Natalie's name. Not that Cade had indicated he thought she was a viable suspect, but I needed to clear my own mind of the things I had heard about her. I knew my niece. She was no killer. But I hated that anyone was even glancing in her direction when there was a murderer that needed to be caught.

WHEN THE FUNERAL WAS over, I had thought I would get a chance to speak to Cade, but he slipped out sometime during the service. I was disappointed. I thought we might get lunch and catch up on what we knew about the case. After dropping my mom and Stormy off at their homes, I thought about Santa's workshop and how someone had to have a key. If no one had seen what happened that meant that whoever had a key would at least be a suspect. I parked my car at the city business office and got out.

"Hi Beth," I said to the receptionist when I entered the office. "How are you doing today?"

She looked up at me and pushed her wire-rimmed glasses up on her nose. "Hi Rainey," she said turning from her computer screen. "I'm doing great. How about you?"

I nodded. "I'm fine. Did you hear about Chrissy Jones?" I whispered the last part. We were in the reception area by ourselves, but I didn't know if any of the offices down the hall had their doors open. I had gone to school with Beth, and at one time we had been close. If she knew something, chances were good she'd tell me.

"Yes I heard," she said looking at me solemnly. "What a terrible shame. Has Cade caught the killer yet?"

I shook my head. "He's working on it night and day. It's just a shame that it happened at Christmas time and right there in the center of town."

"I thought the same thing. Right there in the middle of the Christmas celebrations and everything." She shook her head sadly. "I feel so terrible for her parents. Christmas is a terrible time for anyone to die."

"That's exactly what I was thinking," I said, nodding. "Listen Beth, do you happen to know who may have keys to Santa's workshop?"

"Keys? Let me see," she said thinking about it, and then rifled through a small stack of papers on her desk. She turned and looked at me again. "I know Santa has one and some of the volunteers do."

"Santa?"

She nodded and giggled, and then caught herself and became serious again. "Yes, let's hope Santa didn't kill anyone."

I chuckled. "That would make it worse, wouldn't it?"

She nodded. "Yes, Ned Sanders is Santa Claus in case you didn't know that already. He occasionally has an elf or two to assist him, but I know for sure that Ned has a key."

"Anyone else?"

"Yes, Carolyn at the gift shop across from the fountain has one," she said looking through her papers again. "Oh, and Susan Lang. She was one of the judges for the gingerbread house contest."

That was interesting. "Is that all?"

"Actually, now that I think about it, some of the volunteers also have keys to the workshop. Linda Clarke is in charge of organizing the volunteers, and I know she has one. She also got two extra copies in case she wasn't able to be there when the workshop was open and she needed to send volunteers down to man the shop."

I nodded. That was a lot of people with keys to the workshop. "Tell me, Beth, the workshop wouldn't be left open when no one was there attending to it, would they?"

"To be honest, it shouldn't be. But I did walk up on it a week ago and no one was there. Santa was taking a five-minute break over at the coffee shop and he was without elves that day. One of the volunteers hadn't shown up, and he said he just had to go and get some coffee. He promised me that he was able to see the workshop from where he was." She shrugged. "Let's hope he really could see it. I don't know if its happened at other times or not."

I sighed. That wasn't going to make things any easier. "Let's hope that that was the only time it happened." Even if Ned could see the workshop from the coffee shop, he would have had his back to it while he placed an order, and if the line had been long, he probably hadn't made it back in five minutes like he said.

She nodded. "I was thinking the same thing. But you know how it is. This is Sparrow. Most people are pretty honest and I guess Ned is very trusting."

She was right. We had recently had a string of murders, but that wasn't the norm for Sparrow. During the Christmas season the tourist trade trickled down to almost nothing. There were the cabins down by the Snake River that were sometimes rented at Christmas time. But other than that, there wasn't a lot of tourist traffic and locals tended to trust one another.

"Well Beth, I appreciate the information," I said.

"Anytime Rainey," she said brightly. "I hope Cade finds the killer soon. I hate thinking that we've got somebody wandering around Sparrow that's capable of committing such a heinous crime."

"You and me both," I said. "I'll talk to you later." I turned and left the building. I couldn't imagine anyone leaving Santa's workshop alone for a long period of time. And it didn't seem like the killer would just randomly kill Chrissy and push her body under that table. A murder like this was something that would take some time to accomplish.

Chapter Fourteen

"HEY RAINEY," BILL SEVERS called from across the room.

I looked up from my computer screen. I had been writing an article on coordinating gift wrap and creative gift giving for the newspaper. I worked at the newspaper along with Sam's Diner in hopes of making enough money to make ends meet. I worked both jobs as well as writing my cookbook on the side. "Hey Bill."

He grinned at me. Bill was in his late fifties and was a quiet guy. He didn't say a lot, but there was something about him that I liked.

"Has your boyfriend found out who killed Chrissy Jones?"

I shook my head. "Not yet. But he and the other officers are practically working around the clock to find her killer."

"Seems a shame," he said and looked at his computer screen. "You never know what people are up to in their private lives, do you?"

I eyed Bill. "What do you mean by that?"

He shrugged without looking at me. "I'm just saying that when you mess with the wrong people, you might end up dead."

"Okay Bill," I said. "You can't say something like that and then not tell me what you mean by it. Spit it out."

He looked at me. "I guess I don't really know anything much. But I do know that girl was running around with several different fellas. Could be one of them got tired of being two-timed."

"Would you happen to know the names of said fellas?" I asked. It wouldn't surprise me if it was true, but Cade would want facts and not just rumors.

He shook his head. "No, I've seen her with a young blond guy a few times. And then I heard she was seeing a couple of guys from Boise."

"A couple of guys? And you don't know any names?" I asked again.

He shook his head. "Young blond guy works down at the Sparrow Garage though."

I narrowed my eyes at him. I knew exactly who he was talking about. "Ryan Sparks?"

He thought about it a minute. "That sounds familiar. I think that's his name."

"Do you know how to find any of the other guys she was seeing?"

He shook his head. "No. I wouldn't have even noticed if it weren't for her drawing attention to herself. She was always the loudest person in the room, telling everyone how beautiful and talented she was." He shook his head and chuckled.

"If you hear anything more about any of the guys she was seeing, you'll let me know, won't you?" I thought I really might have to pay Ryan a visit.

He nodded. "I sure will. Even if she was stuck on herself, I hate to see a young girl like that murdered before her life even got started."

"You can say that again," I said.

I finished up my article and kept one eye on the clock. I had a fairly loose schedule when I worked at the newspaper, and not much would have been said if I slipped out early, but I didn't want anyone to think I was a slacker. I hadn't worked there long, and even though I could get an article written quickly, I didn't want anyone to be resentful if I didn't put in my time.

At five o'clock I shut my computer down and gathered up my things. "Okay Bill, I guess I'll see you in a couple of days. I'm off until Thursday."

He nodded. "See you later, Rainey."

I headed out the door of the newspaper office and over to the British Coffee and Tea Company. I hadn't stopped in for several days and I figured Agatha would be wondering where I had been.

I placed an order for a candy cane mocha and a peppermint frost sugar cookie at the coffee shop. It was probably more sugar than I needed to have this time of day, but I was starved. It would probably ruin my dinner, but it was a price I was willing to pay. I picked up my cup of coffee and my cookie and turned around to find a table. I stopped in my tracks. Natalie was sitting at a corner table with Ryan Sparks. That guy really got around. I don't know how I missed them on the way in, but they appeared to be cozily deep in conversation. I probably should have left things alone, but I couldn't do it. I headed over to their table.

"Natalie," I said. "Fancy meeting you here."

Natalie looked up at me and her eyes went wide. She glanced at Ryan and then returned her gaze to me. "Aunt Rainey," she said. "Hi."

I turned to Ryan. "Ryan."

He nodded hesitantly and looked at Natalie. "You know Natalie, I was just getting ready to leave. I've got some errands to run before I go home."

"I hope you're not leaving on account of me," I said.

"Oh no, it's nice to see you again, Rainey. How is your car running?"

"It's running just fine. Thanks for asking," I said without looking at him. I didn't like Ryan. I had been on the fence ever since he had lied to me about his whereabouts when I questioned him about Pamela North's murder. I had just hopped off that fence.

He nodded. "Well, I guess I'll see the two of you later."

"See you later, Ryan," I said and sat down in his seat. I put my mocha and the bag that held my cookie on the table and I looked at Natalie. "What are you doing, Natalie?"

She shook her head slowly. "What do you mean? I was just having coffee with an old friend."

"Really? Because I saw Jenna with him at the Vanilla Bean coffee shop the other night."

Her mouth dropped open. "What do you mean? When did you see him with her?"

I sighed. "Last week. Honestly, Natalie. I'm sure Ryan isn't a terrible person, but it seems like he gets around."

"What do you mean he gets around? Not that it matters. It's not like we're dating. He has a right to hang out with whoever he wants." Her hand went to her necklace, and she twisted the little silver anchor on it.

"Hang out with other people, or date them?" I said and took a sip of my mocha. I didn't want Natalie to get involved with someone like Ryan. He seemed to have a nose for trouble. First there was his deceased girlfriend, Pamela North, and if Bill had it right, he had dated Chrissy as well. Not to mention whatever he was doing with Jenna.

"I'm not dating Ryan. We just went out for coffee," she repeated. She looked away when she said it and I knew she wanted it to be more than just going out for coffee.

"I heard he was dating Chrissy before she died. He was also dating Pamela North."

She looked at me and then looked away. "I didn't know he was seeing Chrissy."

"Natalie, you're an adult now. You have the right to see whoever you want. But I don't think Ryan is going to make you happy. He seems unsure of who he wants to be with."

She looked at me now. "You're right, I am an adult. And I'm going to make the decisions I want to make. I appreciate your concern, Aunt Rainey, but I'm more than capable of making decisions on how I want to live my life," she said firmly.

I nodded. "You're right. Okay. I'll keep my nose out of your business as much as possible, but you have to understand that I care about you and I'll probably never be able to completely mind my own business."

She picked up her cup and took a sip of her coffee before answering. "Fair enough. But as an adult, I might have to remind you of that from time to time."

She tried to suppress a smile when she said it. I knew she didn't want me out of her life, but she was right. I needed to let her make her own decisions or I would drive her away.

"Can I ask you something? Do you have a key to Santa's workshop?"

She shook her head. "No, I've only volunteered a few times. I don't need a key. Why?"

I studied her face. She seemed to be telling the truth. "Where's your cake decorating kit?"

She looked surprised that I had asked. "I meant to ask you about that. I think I left it in the trunk of your car. I'm going to need it to make Christmas cookies."

"It's not in the trunk of my car," I said.

"It isn't?" she said. "I haven't seen it since the contest. I hope I didn't leave it at the high school. I better call them and see if someone turned it in."

"Natalie, it was found near Chrissy's body."

Natalie looked shocked. "Are you sure? It was mine?"

I nodded. "I don't think anyone else would have had a canvas bag with the butterflies and flowers."

"Honestly, Aunt Rainey, I don't know how it could have gotten there. The last place I remember seeing it was when I did those last minute fixes to try to cover that big crack in the back wall of our gingerbread house."

Natalie looked sincere, but it was still unsettling. "That's really the last time you saw it?"

She nodded. "Yes, it's the last time I saw it. I swear, I did not kill Chrissy," she said. Panic was beginning to show in her eyes.

"I know you didn't kill her," I said.

She slowly shook her head and tears sprang to her eyes. "Does Cade think I killed her? I swear I didn't do it!"

I reached a hand across the table and placed it on hers. "Cade knows you well enough to know you aren't capable of killing. It's just weird that it ended up where it did. You said you volunteered that morning, right?"

She nodded. "I met Ryan down there. He had called earlier in the morning and we went to the coffee shop, and then we went and sat down by the fountain. After about a half hour, he left, and I went and played an elf."

I thought about it. "Chrissy really wanted to win that competition and at the same time, beat you. Maybe she stole the decorating kit just to be hateful to you. I don't know how we'd prove it though."

She nodded. "I bet that's it. I don't want Cade thinking I might have killed her. I'd never do that."

"He did say he was going to talk to you, so don't be surprised if he stops by," I said. She needed a warning so she didn't freak out when he questioned her.

Her eyes got big. "He likes me, doesn't he?"

"Oh stop it," I said and lightly slapped her hand. "Of course he likes you. He's just doing his job."

She nodded. "Okay. It's going to be fine."

I took a sip of my coffee. I really didn't know if Chrissy would have taken the decorating kit. I wouldn't have put it past her, but there was no way to know. Maybe the killer wanted to frame Natalie and stole it, leaving it next to Chrissy's body. The canvas bag was distinctive. Everyone would know it belonged to Natalie. The prospect of Cade questioning her made Natalie nervous, and that made me nervous. I would just have to keep the thought of Natalie's innocence foremost in my mind.

Chapter Fifteen

"HI SUSAN," I SAID WHEN I walked through the door to the home interiors store. Susan Lang was the manager there, and I planned on looking for a Christmas gift for my mother as well as see if Susan had anything to add about the gingerbread house decorating contest. I still didn't believe she was telling the truth about not having issues with Chrissy entering the contest.

She smiled brightly. "Good morning, Rainey," she said. "Isn't it a pretty day?"

"It certainly is," I said. "It's so nice after all the gray days we've been having." The weather had cleared up, and the sky was bright blue and sunny. I enjoyed winter days like this. We sometimes went for weeks at a time under gray skies and today was a breath of fresh air.

"Have you got all your Christmas shopping done yet?" she asked, coming out from behind the counter.

"I think I've got most of it done. But I was looking for something special for my mother. She helped me get me into my new house and I want to let her know how much I appreciate it."

"Oh, did you get a new house? How fun!" she exclaimed.

"I did. I moved in a couple of months ago," I said. My eyes fell on a display of birdhouses. There were several that were Victorian-style and I thought it would match my mother's Victorian house nicely. I headed over to the display. "These are lovely."

"Aren't they though?" she said and followed me over. "They've been selling like hot cakes. I bought two of them myself as soon as they came in; a little red barn, and a white Victorian house."

I picked up a yellow Victorian birdhouse and looked at it. "This almost exactly matches my mother's house. I bet she would be thrilled with this." My mother had bought a Victorian house several years earlier and had been gradually restoring it, one room at a time.

"Your mother's house is so lovely. I admire it every time I drive by. She must be so proud of it," she said.

I turned to her. "She really is. She's worked so hard the past few years to return it to its original beauty. Where she's been able to, she's purchased original pieces to put into the house."

"Well, the flower business must be quite lucrative then," she said, smiling. "I didn't realize a florist business would be, but I guess you never know."

I did a double take. Her words seemed to hold a hint of something and I wasn't quite sure what it was. "My mother has worked hard all her life. My sister and I always thought she was a little tight with the money when we were kids, but it certainly has paid off. She's very budget conscious," I said, feeling for some reason that I needed to defend my mother. I chuckled.

"You know how kids are. We didn't understand anything about money. We just wanted what we wanted."

She nodded. "That's completely understandable. Even at my age, I want what I want," she said and laughed. "We also got some new candles in and some beautiful wrought iron and shabby chic chandeliers."

I looked in the direction she indicated and we both walked over to look at them. I held onto the birdhouse. It was absolutely perfect for my mother and I couldn't stand it if somebody stopped in and picked it up before I got a chance to buy it.

"Those are really pretty," I said. And they were. There were wrought-iron chandeliers in various sizes. I looked over the shabby chic ones and decided I liked those the best. Either one would look beautiful in my mother's house, but there was something about the white ones that I really liked. I debated on whether I should get her one of these as well as the birdhouse.

"I have one of these in my foyer. At the entrance to my home, I put up a wonderful farmhouse-style entryway bench and a hall tree. Right above it, I hung one of the shabby chic chandeliers. It's not often that I light the candles, but occasionally I do. Especially now that we're drawing closer to Christmas. I put some red candles in it and I hung some greenery on it. I can't tell you how festive it makes the area look."

"I bet that's really beautiful," I said. "And now that you say that, I can totally see where one of the white ones would be perfect for my mother's house. In fact, it would look lovely in my own house. Maybe I should get one for myself."

She told me the price of the chandelier I had my eye on and I nearly bit my bottom lip to keep from gasping. It was expensive, but my mother had done so much for me this year. Not only had she helped me buy my house, but when I moved home to Sparrow after being away for ten years, I had lived with her for six months.

"It really is pretty. I was amazed at how it brightened up the area. But then, I love Christmas. I decorate nearly every room of my house," she said and chuckled. "My husband used to tell me I was crazy. He couldn't understand why I decorated as I did. His family only had a Christmas tree when he was growing up and he would say that's enough."

"I love Christmas and I love to decorate," I said, still debating on the chandelier. "I'm in the process of rehabilitating my new house, so I only put up a Christmas tree this year. But when I finally get everything done, it would be such fun to decorate all the rooms."

She nodded. "I tried to explain to my husband that it isn't Christmas without all the decorations. He always complained about it, but he was a good sport. He helped me with all of it. I miss my husband so much this time of year," she said and trailed off.

"I'm so sorry," I said. "Has he been gone long?"

"It's been five years now. You would think I would have moved past the grief, but it seems that every time I think I'm finally moving on with my life, a memory of him pops up and the pain just steals my breath away." She shook her head and looked away.

It hurt my heart to hear something like that. I imagined the holidays must be hard for her. "I'm so sorry, Susan," I said. "I know the holidays can be a difficult time for a lot of people."

She nodded and blinked back the tears that threatened to fall. "It really is hard. But I always tell myself that it's better to dwell on the happy memories we made. I wouldn't miss him as much as I do if we hadn't been so happy together. Christmas decorations remind me of him more than anything else." She sighed. "I'm sorry. I don't mean to go on and on about him. What do you think about the chandelier?"

I looked up at it wistfully. "You know what? I think I'm going to get it. It's a lot of money, but I think I'm going to get both the birdhouse and the chandelier for my mom. She'll love them. I'll wait on getting a chandelier for myself. Maybe next year."

"Wonderful," she said and headed over to the front counter. "Let me get a step ladder and I'll get that down for you."

I walked over to the front counter and set the birdhouse down. "I'll have to get some red candles for it," I said and headed over to a display of candles. There were some fat round candles that would work perfectly for the chandelier. I picked up eight of them and brought them back to the front counter.

"You've got to have the candles," she said as she centered the stepladder beneath the chandelier. "Did you want this one?" She pointed to the one I had been standing beneath.

"Yes, that's the one." I wandered back over and stood nearby in case she needed my assistance with anything. "I bet business has been great this time of year."

"It always is this time of year," she agreed. "Say Rainey, have you heard anything new about Chrissy Jones's death?"

"The police are still looking into it. Cade has been working so hard on it, I hardly get to see him these days."

"That's got to be disappointing. I've been thinking it over, and if you want my opinion, I would have a look at her partner, Jenna Dennison." She glanced at me as she worked on the wire that held the chandelier up.

"Oh? Why do you say that?"

She shrugged as she got the chandelier free of its hanger. "Chrissy paid Jenna's entrance fee into the gingerbread decorating contest. You know Jenna's family doesn't have any money. There's no way she could afford it otherwise. Jenna was the whole brains and talent of the team. I overheard them talking and Chrissy said she would do whatever she had to keep your niece Natalie from winning."

I narrowed my eyes at her. "Then when our gingerbread house was broken, why didn't you step in?"

She handed me the chandelier so she could safely climb down the stepladder. "Because I didn't see anything. I had no idea what happened. Just because I suspected something doesn't mean I was right."

That irritated me. Why tell me she overheard them talking and then turn around and not allow Natalie and me extra time to fix the gingerbread house? "I think it would've been a pretty easy guess."

When she got both feet firmly on the floor, she turned to me. "I didn't mean to make you angry. My hands were tied. If I made an exception for you, then others would've wanted me to make exceptions for them."

I had to restrain myself from rolling my eyes. "I can't imagine anybody else needed or wanted an exception. Clearly, we hadn't done anything to cause the damage that was done to our gingerbread house."

She took the chandelier from me and headed to the front counter. "I didn't like Chrissy any more than you do. I thought even with the broken walls of the gingerbread house, yours was prettier. It certainly tasted better."

I followed her over to the front counter. "Then why did Chrissy's house win?"

She went behind the front register and began ringing my purchases up. "Because she came from a wealthy family. Don't you know how things work around here? This town is full of families that have been in this town for generations. The Joneses are one of the oldest families, as well as the wealthiest, and people are not going to vote against the spoiled rich girl."

I stopped in my tracks. I hadn't taken this into consideration. "Why would you think Jenna killed Chrissy?" She'd only told me that she suspected Chrissy and Jenna of cheating, but nothing about why she thought Jenna might have killed her partner.

She hesitated, then continued ringing up the birdhouse. "None of the Joneses are to be trusted. That whole family is no good, regardless of their standing in the community."

"What does that have to do with Chrissy's death?"

She narrowed her eyes. "I heard Jenna hated Chrissy. She only partnered with her so she could have her entrance fee paid, and a person that would partner with someone she hated just to have the money to enter the contest isn't an ethical or moral person."

"I don't know that that's a reason to kill someone."

I knew Jenna's parents had been in and out of jail over the years, but just because they had trouble with the law didn't mean Jenna did. As far as I knew, she had never been in trouble. I did still wonder why the gingerbread house contest was important enough for her to team up with someone she couldn't stand. I hadn't felt she was being truthful when she said she was feeling nostalgic about baking and cake decorating with her grandmother. She had said she had always wanted to compete, and that was her only motivation.

She looked at me and shook her head. "I overheard Jenna on the phone the morning of the competition. She said she was going to take care of the problem and that she and whoever she was speaking to would finally be free. I didn't think much of it at the time, but since Chrissy was killed, I've been thinking it over. The conversation sounded very pointed. Almost like she was speaking on code. Mark my words. Jenna killed Chrissy."

I took a deep breath as Ryan Sparks came to mind.

Chapter Sixteen

CADE LOOKED OVER THE menu in front of him. We were sitting at a booth at the local pizza joint and his stomach growled. "I think they make a mean Hawaiian pizza here." He looked up at me and grinned.

"You sweet talker you," I said and chuckled. "I've been thinking about Hawaiian pizza for days. It's almost like you can read my mind."

"I have skills," he said with a chuckle. He laid his menu on the edge of the table and looked at me. "So, are you all done with your Christmas shopping?"

It was early on a Wednesday night, a few days before Christmas, and the place was nearly empty. I shouldn't have been surprised. Everyone was most likely out getting the last of their Christmas shopping done. I was usually an early shopper, but I had left some of it to finish up this week. I was waiting to get paid, and I was still stumped about what to get Cade. I wanted it to be something special, but I was having trouble coming up with ideas.

"No, you haven't told me what you want for Christmas," I said. "I haven't gotten you anything yet. Is there something special you want? Give me a hint."

He waved the question away. "Your presence all I want. Get it? Presence? It's like presents, only it's presence."

I rolled my eyes. "You're so clever," I said. "But unless you want socks for Christmas, you better tell me what you want." The joke was that I had already bought him some socks. That would be my leading gift on Christmas morning and if he didn't tell me what he wanted, it might end up being his only gift.

"I told you. All I want is you. You can even sing the song if you want."

I rolled my eyes. "The last thing you want for Christmas is me singing to you. I do okay in a group where no one can actually hear me, but you do not want me to sing a solo."

"I mean it," he said. "All I want is you."

He was making things difficult for me. I wanted to get him something special. It was our first Christmas together and I couldn't get him some generic gift. I wanted something that had meaning and that he'd cherish. Or at least something he'd actually use and get some enjoyment from.

Our server arrived at our table, and I was surprised. It was Jenna. I smiled at her. "Hi Jenna," I said. "Are you moonlighting?"

Her eyes went from me to Cade and back again. She smiled, but it was forced. "Hi Rainey," she said, and she nodded at Cade. "I took on a second job. You know how expensive Christmas shopping can get. Do you know what you want yet?"

"I do know how expensive Christmas shopping can get. I think we're going to get a medium Hawaiian pizza and iced tea," I said closing the menu and putting it on top of Cade's menu.

"Great," she said, picking up the menus. "I'll be right out with that."

I looked at Cade. "Did you talk to her?" I asked him.

He nodded. "I did. She seemed intimidated talking to me. Could be my rugged good looks," he said, leaning back in his seat. The red upholstered seat of the booth creaked with the movement.

"I'm sure it was that and not the fact that someone she had partnered with for a recent gingerbread contest had been murdered and the detective on the case was now interviewing her." I raised my eyebrows at him.

He smirked. "I suppose it could have been that," he said. "But I like to think it's my good looks."

"Yes, well, you can think that if you want."

"So what's the plan for Christmas day? Do we open presents first thing? Or the night before?" he asked.

"We usually gather at my mom's Christmas morning and open presents with all the kids. Then we stuff ourselves on an overly sweet breakfast. What do you usually do?" Cade didn't like to talk about past girlfriends or his childhood. He always insisted there wasn't much to tell about his home life growing up. He had lost his mother when he was sixteen and it was something he didn't like to talk about.

"When my mother was alive, we went to church Christmas Eve and opened one gift before we went to bed. We saved the other gifts for Christmas day."

Jenna brought out our iced tea and left without a word. I picked mine up and took a sip. "Needs sugar," I said and opened a packet. "That sounds like fun. I haven't been to church in a while. Maybe we should do that. Make it a tradition?"

"Maybe," he said without looking at me. His eyes were on the fork he was playing with on the table. It made me wonder if I shouldn't have suggested it.

"Or not," I said, hoping he would give me more of an answer.

He looked at me. "It might be fun. We could do that."

"Where have you spent the last few Christmases?" I asked. He had never married, and I wondered if he went home to be with his father and siblings, or if he had stayed with a girlfriend.

"I spent the last two Christmases at the police station in Boise. The one before that, the chief asked me to come to his house."

"Oh. I'm sorry," I said. It made me sad to hear he had been by himself at Christmas time. I thought he would have been with someone that was special to him.

"See?" he said with a smile. "That's why I don't tell anyone about my past. It's full of all sorts of nefarious and mysterious acts. Seriously though, I didn't mind being on my own. Spending the day with the chief was harder. Talk about awkward. But his wife is a sweet woman, and she insisted. She baked the best baklava I have ever tasted. It melted in my mouth."

His smile seemed genuine, but it still seemed sad to me. "Baklava, eh? I've never made one before."

"Maybe it's high time you did?" he said, lifting one eyebrow.

"That could be arranged," I said as Jenna brought out our pizza.

"Here you are," she said, setting it in the middle of the table. "Is there anything else I can get you?"

"I think this will do it," Cade said, sitting up in his seat.

"Great. Enjoy your meal," she said and turned away. She took two steps and then turned back. "Have you found Chrissy's killer yet?" She said it with trepidation and didn't quite make eye contact with Cade.

"We're still working on it," he said, looking at her expectantly. "I'm sure we'll have someone in custody soon."

She nodded. "You know, I was thinking about it and maybe I shouldn't say anything, but I was thinking. I heard that Chrissy framed Elaine Jeffers. They both worked at Michelle's dress shop. Elaine still does. Chrissy framed her for stealing."

"I did hear something about that," I said noncommittally. I didn't want to give away anything specific.

She nodded, not looking at me. Her eyes were glued to a spot on the table in front of her. "It's just that I heard it was actually Chrissy that stole the jewelry. She blamed Elaine because she knew the owner would never believe Chrissy would do something like that. Chrissy didn't have to steal. She had everything she ever wanted."

"Who did you hear that from?" Cade asked.

"Ryan Sparks. He said Chrissy wore the jewelry when they went out, but she said she didn't like it after all. She said she might return it to the store, but later said she could sell it online and make a few dollars off of it."

Ryan Sparks. His name was once again being tossed around. "Does he know for sure that she stole it? She admitted to him that she stole it?" I asked.

She nodded and looked at me now. "She thought it was funny. She couldn't stand Elaine. Said she was beneath her. Chrissy was like that. She didn't think anything of people that didn't have money. I'm surprised she even went out with Ryan. He doesn't come from money." Her chin jutted out on this last part and it made me think she was jealous of the fact that Chrissy and Ryan had dated.

"Did you have problems with Chrissy because she thought you didn't quite measure up?" Cade asked gently. It surprised me he would say it, and I looked at him. His eyes were on Jenna.

Jenna's mouth opened, and it moved without any sound coming out. Then she closed it and gave a curt nod of her head. "Chrissy thought she was better than everyone. And she had no trouble letting you know that when she wanted to."

"Then why did you partner with her?" I asked. "I know you said you really wanted to be in the competition, but it seems like an odd thing to do, considering neither of you liked the other. Why did you really do it?"

Her face paled. "I told you. It was a dream I had. I wanted my grandmother to be proud of me. She taught me everything I know about cake decorating and baking. But my grandmother died a couple of years ago and she never got to see me win."

I wasn't buying it. If I had a history with someone like she did with Chrissy, I'd avoid her like the plague. Life can be difficult enough without going out of your way to be around someone that didn't like you.

"You know, Jenna, if there's something I need to know, it would be good if you told me instead of me finding out on my own," Cade said, sounding stern.

Jenna looked at him, her eyes wide. "It's true that I always wanted to enter the gingerbread competition. I love cake decorating. My grandmother taught me when I was eight and every year we would go and look at the beautiful gingerbread houses together. I promised myself I would get to compete one day," she said. There were unshed tears in her eyes as she talked about the memory. "I never intended to enter with Chrissy, but the entrance fee was so expensive. Chrissy hated Natalie, and she wanted to beat her, so she offered to pay my entrance fee so she could make Natalie feel bad. Against my better judgment, I agreed." She looked at me, her eyes pleading with me to believe her.

"No harm in that I guess," Cade said lightly. "It's good information to have."

"The other thing is, Elaine has a terrible temper. She went into a rage and got into a fight with a girl about six months ago when the other girl stole her boyfriend. She really beat that girl badly. She didn't spend much time in jail, but she was sentenced to anger management classes. She really knows how to hold a grudge."

My eyes went to Cade as he took in this tidbit of information. Whoever had killed Chrissy must have had some anger going on to hit her in the head with a brick. I didn't like Elaine after our conversation where she had implied that Natalie had a good reason to kill Chrissy.

He nodded. "I appreciate the information."

I wasn't completely sure I believed Jenna about wanting to compete in the gingerbread house contest badly enough that she'd partner with someone she hated. But, Elaine Jeffers had just risen up the ranks of suspects. Had she learned to manage her anger after the class she was forced to take or had she let that anger loose and killed Chrissy?

Chapter Seventeen

ELAINE HAD BEEN A COOL customer when I last spoke to her at Michelle's, but sometimes people with anger issues could be calm on the surface. I could see where she might hold a grudge if Chrissy had really set her up like Jenna and Susan had said. It took a lot of nerve to steal from your place of employment and then frame a co-worker. The thing was, I wouldn't put it past Chrissy to do it. She had changed from that cute little blond girl I had known when she was young.

I still wanted to pick up a couple of things for Natalie for Christmas anyway, and I thought I might find some really cute tops for her at Michelle's dress shop.

"Good morning, Elaine," I said when I walked into the shop. She was hanging up sparkly tops that looked more suited to New Year's Eve than Christmas, although I supposed they would work for either. "Those sure are pretty."

She smiled and held up a silver sequined top. "Aren't they though? I really like this one. I might have to buy it with my store discount. I have a New Year's Eve party to go to and this would look so pretty with the black skirt I own."

"I guess with Christmas less than a week away, we can look forward to New Year's now."

"Seems like the season has gone so fast. We also got some cute sparkly bags in," she said indicating a wall with hooks that the handbags hung from. There were some silver ones that would go perfectly with the top.

"Oh, cute!" I said and walked over to the display. "It makes me wish I had a party to go to." I picked up a cute little bag that would only be useful at a fancy party. I could fit my ID, lipstick and money in it and not much else. When I lived in New York, I had spent ten New Year's Eves at parties where this bag would fit in perfectly. Ah, youth.

"You should just go to the one I'm going to. It's being held by Sharon North, at her house. My mom knows her and that's why I was invited, but I heard she was inviting half the town and I'm sure she wouldn't notice an extra person or two," she said amiably.

I was shocked. It hadn't been that long since Sharon North's stepdaughter had been murdered. I couldn't imagine Edward North being in the mood for a party.

"Really? I hadn't heard about it," I said. "She used to work at my mom's flower shop years ago. She and her husband are really nice people. I wonder if her husband will be there?" Edward North traveled frequently on business and it wouldn't surprise me if he would be out of town and that was why his wife was throwing the party so soon after Pamela's death.

She shrugged. "I don't know. Oh, that's right," she said suddenly. "I forgot about Pamela." She tried to suppress a smile when she said it.

I hung the bag up and walked back over to her. "How are things going without Chrissy here? Did Michelle hire a new employee to replace her?"

"Great! Things have gotten so much better around here without Chrissy causing trouble between all the employees. Michelle hasn't gotten around to hiring anyone yet."

"It must be crazy here since it's the Christmas season. With all the shoppers, it must get hectic."

She shook her head. "Not really. To be honest, Chrissy was lazy. She thought she was entitled and entitled girls don't do much work. Besides that, I've picked up more hours with her gone and that's helped me with my own Christmas shopping." She grinned.

I nodded. "You don't miss her at all, do you?"

She looked up from the top she had just hung up. "Not really. I guess that makes me a terrible person in some people's eyes. And maybe I am. But you don't know what it was like working with her. I hated coming to work. She made the day miserably long."

I had my own problem co-worker in Georgia Johnson, but I couldn't imagine being glad if she was murdered. I guess it would be a relief not to have to deal with her on a regular basis, but I could never be happy about it.

"I understand working with someone you don't get along with. But I might be one of those people that can't understand being happy that someone has been murdered." I tried to say it as kindly as I could. I didn't want to alienate her.

She gave me a look that said she wasn't terribly concerned with what I thought. "If it makes you feel any better, I do hope they find her killer. I'd hate for a murderer to be running around Sparrow."

"Can I ask you something?" I said, picking up a gold sequined top. It wasn't Natalie's style. I wasn't sure whose style it would be, because it was unattractive with embroidered roses on the front, but I wanted something to do with my hands.

"Sure. What is it?" she asked as she closed the top on the empty box she had been unpacking the tops from.

"Is it true Chrissy framed you for stealing from this shop?" I watched her face to see if I could read what she was thinking.

The smile left her face, and she stopped what she was doing. "Yes, it's true. That was the kind of person Chrissy was. She'd do something awful and then blame someone else. She was the one who stole the jewelry, not me. Why do you ask?"

I shrugged. "I just wondered. I heard you had a temper and got into some trouble a few months ago. Is that true?" Cade would have a fit if he heard me ask her that, but I wanted to see what her reaction would be. She had insinuated that Natalie had killed Chrissy. I might be holding that against her.

Her cheeks went pink, and she blew air out of her mouth in a huff. "Yeah, it's true. That tramp Jessica Simms was fooling around with my boyfriend. She bragged about it to me and laughed in my face. So you know what I did?"

I shook my head. "No, what?"

"I punched her in her smug face. I did it right in front of everyone when we were at a party because I wanted them to know that I wasn't afraid to stand up for myself. You never know who might have eyes on your man and I didn't want some other tramp to try what she did."

I nodded. "Well, I guess you showed them." I said it in a tone that I hoped conveyed mild approval. I wanted her to continue answering my questions if I needed to come back and ask her anything else.

She nodded, but her cheeks got pinker. "And you know what happened? She called the cops, and I was arrested." She made a noise of disgust. "That stupid judge sentenced me to anger management classes."

"You could have gotten a lot worse," I said.

"Yeah, I know. But now, thanks to the judge, I have better ways of handling my anger issues," she said sarcastically.

"You mean like when someone frames you for stealing?" I asked mildly.

Her eyes went wide. "What? Yes! Like when someone frames me for stealing. Is that what you're getting at? Do you think I killed Chrissy?"

I shrugged. "Did you?"

She sputtered. "No! I had nothing to do with that! Just because I hit someone does not mean I'd kill. Is that what that detective thinks?"

"I have no idea what he thinks. He keeps a lot of the details of his investigations to himself," I said.

She inhaled deeply and paused a moment. I wondered if she had learned this in her anger management class because she suddenly seemed calmer. "I had nothing to do with Chrissy's death. If you want to sniff around someone's heels, why don't you try Susan Lang? She had a really good reason to kill Chrissy."

"What do you mean?" Susan's name was coming up again, but I didn't think she had a plausible reason for killing Chrissy.

"Chrissy's parents bought her house out from under her. She couldn't make the payments on it after her husband died and lost it."

This couldn't be true. Susan had just told me that she had gone all out decorating her house for Christmas. "How do you know that?"

"Because my sister works at the bank that held the mortgage. Susan came in screaming and crying and begging the manager, who just happens to be Carol Jones, to give her more time to find the money to make up the payments she was behind on."

I hesitated, trying to process this. "Are you sure she did that?" I asked. Weren't things like home loans handled at the corporate level? And wouldn't she have had to speak to them if she was losing her home?

She nodded and smiled smugly. "She did. My sister wouldn't make it up. And besides, I saw her at the Hello Motel a few days ago when I was visiting a friend. Her curtains were open and there was a suitcase on the bed."

"Hello Motel?" I asked, puzzled. The Hello Motel was in a rundown part of town. It wasn't a place that anyone would want to stay if they could afford even a little more money.

She nodded. "She's homeless. You tell that to the detective."

"I'll certainly mention it to him." I wasn't sure what to make of this information. It seemed too bizarre to be correct.

She nodded her head triumphantly. "Yes. You go and do that. He needs to talk to her and I think he'll figure out exactly who killed Chrissy."

"How do you know Carol and Roger Jones bought her house out from under her?" I asked.

"Chrissy said they did. She said the house was a dump and thought it was funny that Susan thinks so highly of herself, but she lived in a house that was falling apart and needed a lot of repairs." She shrugged. "That's how Chrissy was. She looked down on anyone that didn't have money. Don't you think that's interesting?"

"Well," I said hesitantly. The look of jubilation on her face as she relayed this information was disconcerting. "Thank you for the information. I guess I'd better get going. I've got to get to work soon."

"You come back and get one of these bags if you're going to the party," she said as she turned away. "And don't forget to tell the detective what I told you."

"Sure I will." I turned and headed out of the shop. I wasn't convinced about what she had told me. I couldn't see Susan living at a seedy motel.

Chapter Eighteen

I DIDN'T KNOW WHAT to think about what Elaine had said about Susan. She had been so excited and sentimental about Christmas when I spoke to her that I could hardly believe she was homeless and living in Sparrow's worst motel. The Hello Motel was run down and whenever I had driven past it, there were some shifty looking characters hanging around out front. Which made me wonder what kind of friend Elaine had been visiting.

"What did you bring us today?" Sam asked, peering at the shopping bag I held in my hand.

"An eggnog cheesecake. What's more Christmassy than that?" I asked as I removed it from the bag and set it on the kitchen counter.

"Oh, that sounds good," Luanne said, leaning over my shoulder. "Can you get drunk from eating it?"

I looked at her. "Seriously? Have you lived under a rock all your life, Luanne?"

"I have not! I just don't know what you put in an eggnog cheesecake."

"The cheesecake is baked and if there *was* alcohol in it, which there isn't, the alcohol would cook off in the heat of the oven," I explained, removing the lid. "The snow is keeping people home so we'll have plenty of time to sample this."

"Thank goodness," Diane said, walking into the kitchen. "My feet are killing me. I spotted that bag when you came in. What is it?"

"Eggnog cheesecake," I said. "Want a slice?"

"Are you kidding? Don't stand there and ask me a dumb question like that and get to cutting."

I chuckled. "I take it you all have been waiting for me to bring something in to sample?" I asked.

"You better believe it," Ron White, our dishwasher said. "I was just telling Sam he needed to let you go. You've been slacking."

"Thanks a lot, Ron," I said and went to a cupboard and got some plates down. "I used real heavy cream, just so you all know if you're watching your weight."

Sam groaned. "I don't watch my weight until sometime in January. Preferably the end of January."

"Right?" Diane asked him. "Calories don't count in December, anyway."

"I'm with you both," I said.

I cut everyone a piece and put it on the plates while Diane hung near the kitchen door in case we got some customers. The cheesecake had turned out perfectly creamy, and I was pleased. I had worried the top might crack while baking.

"Oh my gosh, this is perfect," Diane groaned when she had taken a bite. "The nutmeg really brings out the eggnog flavor."

"Wow," Sam said, nodding his head.

"I guess that means I have your approval?" I asked.

Sam nodded. "Best cheesecake I've ever tasted. I'm sure glad it's Christmas time, and this stuff is in season."

I heard the bell over the front door jingle. "I'll get it. You all enjoy yourselves." I headed to the front counter and saw Cade sitting there. "Hey, baby."

He grinned. "I don't think you've ever called me baby before."

"Well it's high time I did," I said and gave him a quick kiss. Then I gave him one not so quick. There weren't any other customers in the diner, so I did it guilt-free.

"How are things with you?" he asked.

"Great. I brought cheesecake. Let me get you some."

"Do I have perfect timing, or what?"

I headed back to the kitchen and cut him a piece and then stopped to pour him a cup of coffee on my way back. "Here we are." I set the plate and the cup of coffee in front of him.

"Looks good," he said and took a big bite. "Wow, really good!"

I chuckled. "I'm glad you approve."

He took another bite and his phone went off. He sighed and pulled it from his pocket. When he'd read the text, he shook his head and sighed. "As much as I'd love to finish this wonderful piece of deliciousness, I've got to get back to the station."

"Is everything okay?" I asked.

.

"Most likely. You know how the chief is. He can't seem to explain things with a phone call or a text."

"Oh?" I asked.

"He's old fashioned. He's got to talk to people face-to-face." He got to his feet and looked longingly at the cheesecake. Then he took another quick bite. "Save me some?" he said around the food in his mouth.

"You got it," I said as he left the diner.

A minute later Carol and Roger Jones came through the door. I smiled. "Hello, Carol, Roger. Would you like a booth?"

"That would be great," Carol said.

I picked up two menus and showed them to a nearby booth and took their drink orders. I went to get them an iced tea and a diet Coke. I tried to think of a way to ask them about Susan. The more I thought about it, the more I thought Elaine couldn't be telling the truth.

"Here we are," I said, bringing the drinks back to their table. "Would you like more time to decide?"

"No, I'm ready. I'd like the clam chowder," Roger said.

I pulled my order book from my apron pocket and jotted down his order and waited for Carol to make up her mind.

"I'm debating between the clam chowder and a big juicy burger. Sam makes such tasty burgers and I've been thinking about them all day, but I don't need the calories. Not that the clam chowder would save me calories, it's so thick and rich."

"Now, you know that calories don't count from Thanksgiving through New Year's Day," I reminded her.

She chuckled. "You're right. I'll take the teriyaki burger."

"You got it," I said, writing down her order. I wanted to ask them about Susan's house, but I didn't know if it might seem odd. "How are you two doing?" I asked after I finished writing. I was trying to find a way to ask what I needed to know.

Roger sighed. "We're coping as best we can."

"This is the first day we've left the house. I just don't want to do anything," Carol said with a hitch in her voice.

"I can't imagine how hard this has to be," I said.

"I don't know what's taking the police so long to figure out what happened to our little girl," Roger said gruffly. "Seems like they should have had this figured out already."

"I know Cade is doing everything he can to find your daughter's killer. I'm so sorry."

He nodded without looking at me. "Chrissy was loved by everyone that knew her. I don't know why this happened."

"I think it had to be someone on drugs," Carol said, looking at me. "I told Cade that. He needs to look at some of the young people around here. I think someone was at a party and used drugs and maybe killed her on accident."

"That's a possibility," I said. "Can I ask you both something?"

They nodded and looked at me expectantly.

"Did you all buy Susan Lang's house?" It was a question that probably seemed out of the blue to them and I hoped they didn't press me on why I was asking.

"Yes. A little over a month ago. It was sold at auction after the bank foreclosed on it. Why?" Roger asked.

"Really? I had no idea it was foreclosed on. I could have sworn she was still living there."

Carol shook her head. "That woman. She is something else. Home loans are handled in our main office and I know for a fact that they give a person every opportunity to keep their home. I saw the house was on the list of local foreclosures and it was in such a great location that I told Roger we needed to grab it when the foreclosure went through. You could say we had an inside advantage."

"We've gotten a lot of great deals that way," Roger added.

"But when we bought the house, Susan came to us and asked us to sell it back to her. She wanted us to carry the papers on it. When we told her we couldn't do that, she asked us to rent it to her. There was no way we were doing that. The place was a mess when we finally got to go inside of it. It was in need of a lot of repairs too, and we weren't going to rent it to someone that treated a home like that," Carol said.

"Besides that, I buy homes to refurbish them and sell at a profit. That house has water damage and needs new electrical put in it. I'm barely going to make a profit after all the clean up and repairs. There's no way I was going to rent it to her. I don't buy houses to do charity work," Roger said and snorted.

I nodded. Poor Susan was either delusional about decorating her house, or too embarrassed to admit she had lost it. Financial troubles could make a person do desperate things, but could they make someone kill?

"That's a shame," I said. "It must have been a stressful thing to go through. Losing a house."

"Why do you ask, Rainey?" Carol asked me.

I shrugged. "I knew Roger was in real estate and I just wondered if that was one of the houses you all bought. It's in a nice, older neighborhood. I bet it will sell quickly."

"It is in a good location," Roger said. "You know what they say. Location, location, location. It should be the most important factor when you buy a house."

"I agree. I recently bought a house, and it's in a nice quiet neighborhood," I said.

I sighed inwardly at having dodged that question. Poor Susan. That house and its memories had been important to her. Losing a house is tough. Losing a house during the holidays is tougher. But would it be enough to cause her to make the Joneses lose something that meant even more to them?

Chapter Nineteen

CHRISTMAS EVE DAWNED clear and bright and it gave me a warm feeling in spite of the brisk cold air. I had the day off from the diner and the newspaper was closed. It was going to be a wonderful day. I had stayed up late the night before and gotten all the presents wrapped and they were sitting prettily beneath my Christmas tree. Cade and I had plans to attend a church service in the evening and then we'd drive around town and look at Christmas lights. Chinese takeout would follow that up, and then we'd relax in front of the fireplace and sip cocoa. I could pinch myself. It felt like I was finally living the life I had always dreamed of.

I had high hopes for the coming year. I was almost finished writing my cookbook, and I had been promised a few more hours at the newspaper. I still wanted to write more than lifestyle articles, but I did enjoy what I was doing. If I could wrangle a publishing contract for my cookbook, I might be able to pay back the money I had borrowed from my mother for the down payment on my house. I sighed. The new year was going to be wonderful with Cade in my life. If someone had told me at the beginning of this year, things would turn around for me as they had, I would have said they were crazy.

But, I couldn't get what the Joneses had said about Susan Lang and her house out of my mind. I also couldn't get what Susan had said about decorating her house for Christmas out of my mind, either. She had had me convinced it was true.

Cade was at the police station and I had time to kill until he got off work, so I got into my car and drove around town. The season had gone so quickly and it wouldn't be long before all the lights were taken down and we'd be back to our regular world. It had snowed two days earlier, and it had stuck, making Sparrow look like a winter wonderland. We still hadn't gotten around to building the snowman that Cade said he wanted to build, but if he got off work early enough, maybe we could fit it in before the church service.

I thought I would stop in at the British Coffee and Tea Company and get what would probably be my last candy cane mocha of the season as well as say hello to Agatha. But as I was driving, I couldn't get Susan Lang living at the Hello Motel out of my mind. Elaine hadn't said what room she saw Susan in, so it probably wouldn't do me any good to go by there, but it wouldn't hurt either.

I pulled into the parking lot and sat with my engine idling, taking it in. The motel needed a good cleaning and a fresh paint job. It wasn't a place I would want to stay. I turned the engine off and looked around the parking lot, but I didn't know what kind of car Susan drove.

As I watched, a maid pushed her cleaning cart into a room. A couple of kids came out of the room and scampered about in the parking lot. They looked to be about eight and nine and they had a small ball they bounced to each other. The ball got away from the boy and both he and his sister ran after it. It bounced beneath a dark blue sedan and they knelt beside it to take a look for it. It made me sad that these kids would be spending Christmas in this motel. I hoped they would benefit from the toys donated to Santa's workshop and that it wouldn't be a disappointing Christmas for them.

As I watched the kids hunt for the ball beneath the car, my eyes fell on the license plate. SUSNLNG. It was personalized and must have meant something to the owner, and I tried to come up with what it might mean. I don't want to brag, but I figured out it must mean 'Susan Lang' in under three minutes. Some days I wasn't real quick.

It was parked in front of room number eight. The blinds were drawn, and I wondered if I should go up and knock on the door. What would I say to her? 'Surprise! I came to see your Christmas decorations'? That hardly seemed appropriate. I bit my lower lip. I could knock on the door and say I was looking for a friend, but no one I knew would want to stay at this motel.

After a few minutes, I took a deep breath and decided to do it. I could tell her I saw her go into the motel. I could tell her I wanted to invite her to my family's Christmas dinner the following day. I didn't know Susan all that well, but it was Christmas and everyone was doing things they don't normally do at other times of the year. It was sad that a lot of people didn't do more charitable things all year, but it was true, nonetheless. Maybe I could also invite the kids and whoever they lived with. I watched as the maid came out of room nine and the kids went back inside. Whatever she had done in there, it wasn't a thorough cleaning.

I got out of my car and went to the door of room eight and knocked. When Susan opened the door, her eyes went wide. She stood, her mouth open in surprise.

I smiled. "Hi, Susan," I said and waited to see what she would say once the surprise wore off.

"Hi, Rainey," she said slowly. "I wasn't expecting anyone."

"Sorry to just pop over here like this, Susan," I said. She was dressed in gray sweats, a white t-shirt, and a ratty pink bathrobe. "I was just in the neighborhood."

Her eyes went behind me, scanning the parking lot, and she pulled her robe around herself. "I have to go to work soon," she said and took a small step backward, making a move to close the door.

"Susan, I know this is awkward, but I wondered about tomorrow. If you don't have any plans, would you like to come to my house for Christmas dinner?" It sounded lame, even in my own ears. We both knew things weren't right here.

She looked at me, the surprise not fully gone from her face. "That's so sweet of you—I have plans though." She nodded in an attempt to convince me.

"Oh," I said. "Okay. Well, I just thought I'd stop by and ask."

"I—I don't live here." Her face was turning pale.

"Oh? Oh, of course not," I said and waited.

She licked her lips. "My house is being painted. It was a mess. I didn't want to get in the worker's way, you know, so I decided to stay at a motel for a few days. I should have thought things through before scheduling the painters to come so close to Christmas." She shrugged and tried to laugh it off.

I nodded. "Of course." I didn't know what to do next. Had I just humiliated a woman that was trying her best to survive a tough situation? And then I thought I better get down to business. I really wouldn't mind her coming to Christmas dinner. It was the least I could do. "It's tough, losing a home this time of year. I'm sorry."

Tears sprang to her eyes, and she gave a short nod of her head. "It is. But, things will get better. I know they will."

"Of course. You're still more than welcome to come to dinner."

"I'll be okay. Everything will work out." She forced herself to smile.

"I'm sure it will," I said. "Sometimes things don't turn out as we'd planned. I know that feeling. I thought I'd be married to my ex-husband for the rest of my life."

She opened her mouth to say something, then closed it. I waited while she came up with what she wanted to say.

"It's a shame that those with money feel they can take advantage of the less fortunate, especially this time of year," she finally said and nearly choked with the bitterness in her voice. "But you know how it is. Karma never lets the guilty go free."

"What do you mean?" I asked, hoping she would say more.

"You know, an eye for an eye," she said with a smirk.

"You mean a daughter for a house?" I asked.

"Whatever it takes," she said through gritted teeth.

"A house doesn't compare to a human life," I pointed out. There were butterflies in my stomach and now I wished I had waited to talk to Cade about this before coming here.

"I find that when you commit one evil act, the act that comes back to you is worse than what you did. It's the way the world works. Haven't you figured that out by now?"

I shook my head. "What a terrible way to think," I said. I took a step forward and placed my foot against the door. My phone was in my pocket and I pulled it out.

She shoved me, and I lost my grip on my phone as it flew out of my hand. She pulled a knife from her robe pocket and my eyes went to it. It was a serrated steak knife with a cheap plastic handle.

"It's a terrible neighborhood, and it's all I have to protect myself," she explained with a grin. "Let's go for a drive."

I backed up, keeping an eye on the knife and she stepped outside her room. She reached back and locked the door, then fished her car keys from her pocket.

I stepped back again and without a word, I kicked her arm with all my might. I had recently returned to the gym and my kickboxing skills were in full form. She screamed, and the knife flew from her hand. I kicked her again, this time in the thigh and she dropped to her knees with a scream.

"You broke my leg!" she howled.

I was sorry to see the door to room number nine open, and a woman looked out, the two kids peeking out from behind her. I didn't want the kids to see this.

"It's okay," I assured them and went to where my phone had landed. While Susan cried and cussed me, I picked up my phone and called Cade.

Susan shrieked again and told the woman I was assaulting her and asked for help. "The only help I'm giving is calling the police," the woman said and slammed her door.

I dialed Cade and told him Susan Lang had killed Chrissy. Christmas would never be the same for a lot of people, but especially for the Joneses and Susan Lang.

Chapter Twenty

IT DIDN'T TAKE MUCH to take Susan down. She wasn't in great shape and I had caught her off guard. If the motel hadn't been in such a lousy part of town, she wouldn't have had that knife in the pocket of her robe and might not have even tried anything.

The woman in room nine had done what she said she was going to do. She dialed 911. Cade and the police were there at the motel within minutes. While we waited, the maid came out of room ten and helped me keep Susan there in the parking lot by spraying her face with antibacterial cleaner. Having been far more dramatic than necessary about a supposed broken leg, she had tried to limp over to her car to make a getaway. I threatened to give her another kick, this time to her head, and that helped convince her to stay put. Kick boxing classes came in handy.

I had invited the woman with the children in room nine at the Hello Motel to Christmas dinner, but she had declined. I think I might have scared them a little when I kicked Susan in the leg. She had assured me that the children had received some donated toys and they had plenty of food. There was a small Christmas tree in their window and wrapped presents beneath it, so I let it go. Life could be hard, but it seemed that she had taken care of what mattered to the kids at Christmas. I wished them well and came home to wait for Cade.

Cade and I had missed the church service we had planned to attend, and it was nearly eleven o'clock by the time he got free after questioning Susan. That meant no Christmas lights or Chinese food, either. Everything was closed up tight by the time he got to my house, so I whipped up grilled cheese sandwiches and a piece of leftover Noel cake. But now we were finally sitting in front of that roaring fire, snuggled up together on the sofa with a cup of cocoa. It was cozy, and I was sleepy, but the Christmas tree was so pretty by the light of the fire. I leaned my head on Cade's shoulder and closed my eyes. My dog Maggie dozed with her head on Cade's shoes, having enjoyed several bites of his grilled cheese sandwich.

"Do I have to tell you that I want you to stay out of trouble?" Cade murmured. He had held back and so far wasn't complaining about me asking suspects if they had murdered anyone recently.

"No, I've heard it enough," I said sleepily.

"Good. I'm tired of saying it. I just wish you'd listen."

I chuckled. "My mother didn't have any more success at getting me to eat my vegetables than you have in keeping me out of trouble. Still, it's a shame. Chrissy is dead because of a foreclosed house. I mean, I get that it's an awful thing to have happen, but it isn't worth anyone's life."

"Nope. Sure isn't."

"I don't get why she blamed the Joneses. They just bought the house at auction," I mused.

"She said when her negotiations with the bank failed, and the Joneses bought her house, she tried to buy the house back from them. When they refused, she tried to rent it from them. She was angry and bitter when they refused. But then she changed her story, saying she never missed any house payments, and that Carol Jones arranged for her to lose her home so she and her husband could buy it. I guess the frustration built up, and she decided to take something they loved from them," he said and took a sip of his cocoa.

"When I stopped in at the store, she went on and on about how she had decorated every room in her house for Christmas and her late husband thought she was going overboard. She sounded as if she still lived there and I honestly thought that was true. I think the grief of losing her husband must have played into it all. Losing her husband and then the house where they had made so many happy memories drove her over the edge."

"She did in fact say she felt like she was losing her husband all over again," he said. "Sad."

"It really is. Do you ever feel bad when you arrest people that have a sad story behind why they did what they did?" I asked him.

"If I did, it would affect my ability to do my job. Sure, it's sad that she lost her husband and her home, and it's very sad the loss of the house was during the holiday season. But, losing a daughter far outweighs any pain she experienced in losing the house. The Joneses have to live with that for the rest of their lives."

I sighed. There was no easy way out of either of these situations. "I wish things could have turned out differently."

"Me too."

"How did she do it?"

"She stewed over losing the house and decided that Carol and Roger should lose something dear to them as repayment for stealing her house, as she puts it. She was angry that Chrissy won the gingerbread house decorating contest and it occurred to her that it would be fitting to kill Chrissy and stick her under the table that held the winning entries."

"That's really twisted," I said.

"Isn't it though? She lured Chrissy to the workshop with Natalie's cake decorating kit. She thought Chrissy would be petty enough to want it just so Natalie couldn't have it, so she stole the kit. She was right. Chrissy fell for it and met her there after hours where Susan hit her on the head with a brick."

I sighed. "That's just nuts."

"It is indeed."

I sat for a few minutes, taking this in. Then I looked at him. "Hey, why don't we open the traditional Christmas Eve present? It's still Christmas Eve for a couple more minutes," I said, getting up and heading to the tree. I had bought Cade several presents, and I still wasn't sure I had done a very good job figuring out what to get for him. But there was one thing I thought he was going to enjoy. I picked up a present from beneath the tree and brought it to him.

He eyed me. "Your present is at my apartment. We can wait until tomorrow."

"No. It's tradition and traditions are important," I said and handed him the gift. I decided the socks could wait. I wanted to see his reaction to what I had bought for him.

He smiled, but it was tinged with sadness. I hoped I hadn't brought up sad memories for him. He took it from me and slowly began unwrapping the paper, a pretty design with a white background and red glittery Christmas bells on it.

When he tore open the paper enough to see what was in it, he looked up at me and gave me a genuine smile. "You are something else."

"Thank you," I said and sat beside him again.

"I've wanted an Orvis fly-fishing rod for a while now. I haven't gone fly-fishing in years."

"I'm glad you like it," I said. "I wasn't sure if it was something you'd like, but I thought I'd take a chance since you've been hinting to me for months now that you wanted to go fishing."

"And now we're going to have to get you a rod so we can go together," he said.

I groaned. "I was hoping you might find a friend to go with you. Maybe Sam or Bob?"

He shook his head. "The couple that fishes together stays together. I can't wait until the weather warms up a little so I can try this baby out."

I chuckled. Cade might look like a city slicker in the suits he wore for work, but he was an outdoorsman at heart. I wasn't sure I wanted to be an outdoorswoman with him, but I had an idea that I was probably going to be, whether I wanted to or not. It was fine though. Any time I got to spend with him was wonderful.

The End

Sneak Peek

FISH FRY AND A MURDER
   A Rainey Daye Cozy Mystery, book 9
   Chapter One

"We're going to catch our death of cold out here," I said, trying to keep the whine out of my voice. The sun was just starting to peek its head over the horizon and the blowing wind had my nose running. I rubbed the back of my gloved hand beneath it. I wasn't a morning person under the best of circumstances.

Cade chuckled. "You'll be fine. As soon as the sun is up, you'll warm right up." He hefted the ice chest from the trunk of his car and set it on the frozen ground. "There's nothing like time spent in the great outdoors."

"I don't think I'll warm right up," I grumbled and picked up the two canvas folding chairs from the trunk. It was early January in Idaho and all I wanted was to hide beneath my electric blanket and sleep the morning away. A girl could dream, right?

"Come on, be a trooper. I know you can do it," he teased and led the way to the edge of the lake. "We'll have a mess of fish caught before you know it and then you can stand in front of a roaring campfire and fry them up for us."

"Yeah, that sounds like fun," I said and yawned.

"At least the fire will warm you up," he said over his shoulder.

I stumbled after him, my thick layers of clothing making me feel less than graceful. We stopped at the edge of the frozen lake and Cade looked it over.

"What if it doesn't hold us?" I asked. I had never been ice fishing, and I didn't think I would enjoy it. Mostly because it involved ice and bitterly cold temperatures. I had spent all of my life in snowy areas, first Idaho, then New York, and now back to Idaho, but I had never really embraced cold weather activities. At least, not when they occurred outdoors.

"It'll hold. I hear there've been a lot of trout pulled out of this lake this season." He set the ice chest down and headed back to the car for his fishing equipment.

I unfolded the two chairs and set them on the ground, then sat down in one. I pulled my knit hat down lower over my ears and re-wrapped my scarf. My eyes began to tear up from the wind and I blinked to clear them and sniffed.

"Hey, what are you doing sitting down?" Cade asked, returning with a tackle box the size of a small safe, two fishing poles, and an auger to drill holes into the ice.

I looked up at him. "I like the feel of solid earth beneath my feet. I think we should fish from right here on the bank."

He chuckled and shook his head. "How are we going to do that? The lake's surface is frozen solid. You can't cast your line out and expect it to do anything other than bounce across the ice."

I shrugged. "Just drill a hole a couple of feet out. I bet I can cast the hook into it from here."

"If I drill a hole a couple of feet from the bank, the water beneath it will only be a few feet deep. The fish aren't hanging out in the shallow water just waiting for us to catch them. Where's your sense of adventure?"

"My sense of adventure abandoned ship when it saw we were headed out into the cold. What if the ice doesn't hold us? I've seen videos of people falling through the ice and freezing to death before they can climb out," I protested.

"You've seen real people die in these videos?" he asked skeptically. "Or are you talking about when you watched *Titanic*?"

"I am not talking about *Titanic*. I saw real people. I guess they probably didn't actually die, but did you know you can freeze to death in icy water in less than fifteen minutes?"

He laughed and shook his head, taking a few steps out onto the ice, then bent over and used the manual auger to quickly drill a hole. "There. See? The ice is nice and thick. Come on out and bring those chairs. I've got ice to drill and fish to catch."

I sighed, got to my feet, and folded the chairs up again. The ice did look thick, and it wasn't that I doubted Cade, but I didn't like the idea of walking out onto that ice. Cade had bought me a pair of ice boots so I wouldn't slip, and I had put on two pair of socks to keep my feet warm, but they weren't working very well. My feet were freezing. I had also worn two layers of thermals beneath my clothes and I felt like the kid on *A Christmas Story* when his mother made him wear that absurd snowsuit. I drew a line at the ridiculous looking bib overalls Cade was wearing.

They were bright orange and apparently waterproof. A girl's got to keep her sense of fashion even when ice fishing.

I looked up as Cade continued walking further out onto the ice. "Hey! Don't go so far out."

He turned and waited as I gingerly made my way onto the ice. I paused at the hole he had just drilled and looked into it. The ice appeared to be at least four inches thick. I strained my ears for cracking sounds, but the ice was blessedly silent.

"Come on. The big fat fish are out in the deep," he called. "I want to catch the really big ones. Go big or go home."

"I'll take little skinny fish if it means I can stay on the shore," I said as I braced myself and headed slowly in his direction. "Going home now would be even better."

"Live a little, Rainey. Look on the bright side. If we do fall in, you'll have something to tell our grandchildren."

I gasped and looked at him, then looked back at my feet. I didn't have any children, let alone grandchildren. Cade and I had only been dating a few months, but I had never been so happy in all my life. I had come off of a nasty divorce a year earlier and I swore I would never fall in love again, and yet, here I was. Not that I was admitting I was in love. Not yet, anyway. But sometimes, out of the blue, Cade would say something like he had just said, and I'd think, this is it. This is the real thing. The love I have waited for my whole life. As these thoughts passed through my mind, my foot slipped on the ice and I gasped again and put the folding chairs down on the ice, using them as a crutch to keep me upright.

"You okay?" he called. He had ventured further out onto the ice and I wished he would just stay put.

I looked up and smiled as the sun rose behind him. He looked stunning in the early morning light, silly overalls and everything. "I'm okay."

I made my way out to where he had set the tackle box down and begun drilling a hole in the ice. Unfolding the chairs, I set them several feet away from the hole. I had visions of my weight adding to the stress of holes being drilled into the ice and my ever-creative imagination saw us both falling into the treacherous water beneath the ice.

He glanced at me. "I can't sit in the chair with it so far way." He moved over to a spot about eighteen inches from the hole he had just drilled and made another one. The auger was amazingly quick in drilling holes into the ice.

I scooted the chairs closer once he was finished with the second hole. "We could just go to the grocery store and buy some fish."

"Once again, where's your sense of adventure? Besides. I bought these spiffy overalls. It would be a waste of money not to wear them."

"Yeah, I can see why you'd want to wear them. Everyone from Sparrow to Boise can see them."

He snorted. "These overalls are like your little black dress on date night. Would you want to dress up and stay home where no one can see you?"

"Well, when you put it like that," I said and sat down on my chair.

"Exactly. Now, what kind of bait would you like on your hook? I've got big fat nightcrawlers, minnows, and stinky marshmallows."

I looked at him. "I don't want to appear to be a greenhorn, but are the nightcrawlers and minnows alive?"

"Of course. The fish like their breakfast to have a little game. Makes them friskier." He opened his tackle box and began sorting through it.

"I was afraid of that. I'll take stinky marshmallows." I sat back in my chair and watched the sunrise. It was eerily quiet out on the lake and if it hadn't been so cold, I might have enjoyed it.

"I'll bait our hooks and then go get the ice chest," he said as he removed the lid from a jar of fluorescent pink marshmallows.

I peered at the ice beside me. The wind had blown most of the snow off of the lake's surface and I could see through it. It was a little unnerving as I saw what looked like a fish dart beneath me.

"This is really weird," I said. "What if I fall through the ice? I mean, seriously. Do we have a plan?"

"Stop it. You aren't going to fall." He handed me the baited fishing rod. "Now, all you really have to do is put the hook into the hole and wait for the fish to bite. Maybe move it around a little. I put a float on it. Trout like to stay somewhat near the surface and like to see their food float. I'll be right back."

I watched as he headed back for the rest of our equipment, then turned back to the hole in the ice. I got to my feet and peered into it, trying not to get too close to the edge. A small fish darted across the opening and I jumped a little. If Cade thought he was going to get nice fat fish, he might be mistaken. The two I had seen so far were far from large. I dropped the hook into the water, releasing some line, then scooted back to my chair and sat and waited.

Buy Fish Fry and a Murder on Amazon:

https://www.amazon.com/Fish-Fry-Murder-Rainey-Mystery-ebook/dp/B07P4MQGVC

IF YOU'D LIKE UPDATES on the newest books I'm writing, follow me on Amazon and Facebook:

https://www.facebook.com/Kathleen-Suzette-Kate-Bell-authors-759206390932120/

https://www.amazon.com/Kathleen-Suzette/e/B07B7D2S4W/ref=dp_byline_cont_pop_ebooks_1

Made in United States
North Haven, CT
02 June 2024

53232498R10098